"Is someone courting you?" Arden asked.

"That's a brazen question." It was also a question that stung a little bit.

"I was just…" His face colored. "Sorry, I was curious. I thought someone would be… I mean…"

His embarrassment softened her. "No, I don't have anyone special at the moment, not that it's your business. But we do have a quality matchmaker here in Redemption, and as my *mammi* points out, I've got some marriageable qualities. So I don't think it's being too prideful to expect to find a husband."

Besides, Sarai had faith that *Gott* would bring the right man along…hopefully soon, and very possibly in Shipshewana.

"You'll have no problem at all." Arden shot her a lopsided smile that made her breath catch. He'd always been a charmer.

Arden had also always irritated her. While the other girls in Redemption swooned at his smiles and got their hearts broken by this too-smooth and too-handsome man, Sarai had seen him for what he was—selfish. It was a game for him, and she refused to ever fall for the likes of Arden Stoltzfus.

Patricia Johns is a *Publishers Weekly* bestselling author who writes from Alberta, Canada. She has her Hon. BA in English literature and currently writes for Harlequin's Love Inspired and Heartwarming lines. She also writes Amish romance for Kensington Books. You can find her at patriciajohns.com.

Visit the Author Profile page at LoveInspired.com for more titles.

The Amish Marriage Arrangement

Patricia Johns

LOVE INSPIRED
INSPIRATIONAL ROMANCE

LOVE INSPIRED®

INSPIRATIONAL ROMANCE

Recycling programs for this product may not exist in your area.

ISBN-13: 978-1-335-59678-9

The Amish Marriage Arrangement

For questions and comments about the quality of this book, please contact us at CustomerService@Harlequin.com.

Love Inspired
22 Adelaide St. West, 41st Floor
Toronto, Ontario M5H 4E3, Canada
www.LoveInspired.com

Printed in U.S.A.

Let all your things be done with charity.
—*1 Corinthians* 16:14

To my husband and son. I love you both so much! You are the happiest part of every day.

Chapter One

Sarai Peachy's grandmother sat at the kitchen table with a ledger in front of her. She squinted at the small print, a pen in hand.

"You don't have to do that, Mammi," Sarai said. "I can take care of it."

"It's all right, dear," Mammi Ellen replied. "We're getting more customers now with your hens. We've got Englisher orders coming in faster than we can fill them. That's a blessing, you know."

Blessings often come dressed like hard work. That was what her late Dawdie Jacob used to say, and Sarai smiled at the memory. There was a sign at the road that read *Peachy Eggs—Marans, Easter Eggers, Ameraucanas, Light Sussex, Olive Eggers. Inquire at the house.* A sign at the road was enough to bring in customers so far, and word of mouth had spread the news of their colorful, organic, free-range eggs.

In fact, Sarai's cousin Katie had been asking Sarai's advice on how to grow her own flock of hens that would produce such varied eggs as well, and in the last few letters they'd exchanged, Katie had come up with an idea. Sarai's Aunt Lovie and Uncle Jonah in Shipshewana were opening their home to tour groups and giving buggy rides. Katie was selling eggs and offering tours of the coops. They were finding more success than they'd imagined, and they needed someone to help out with running the place. Why not Sarai? Katie asked.

It was an intriguing offer. It would use Sarai's skills as well as put her in a new community to meet available young men... Except, she was staying with Mammi Ellen because Mammi needed the help more urgently. Mammi loved her house, and she couldn't take care of it alone anymore. If Sarai went to Aunt Lovie and Uncle Jonah's house, Mammi would never be able to continue on her own. She'd have to move in with family somewhere, and it would break her heart. Although, an idea had started to stir...

"We have three more people on our waiting list for regular orders," Mammi Ellen said. "You've really gotten this egg business off the ground, dear girl."

Sarai Peachy stood at the counter, placing the afternoon's freshly washed eggs into cartons. She'd been raising a variety of different hens ever since she was a girl, and she now had a flock of birds that were not only good layers but also produced a beautiful array of different-colored eggs, from creamy white to blue, green, speckled and even a coppery brown. She'd found that eggs sold best when arranged with complementary colors in the cartons—copper and dark green together, for example, or pale blue, mint-green and brown-speckled eggs in another carton.

Sarai looked out the kitchen window, and she spotted

their elderly neighbor, Moe, on his way over. He walked with a stick, his wiry white hair jutting out from under his hat. A young man followed a few paces behind, and Sarai paused in her work and squinted.

"Moe is on his way over," Sarai said. "He's almost at the garden."

"Oh, good," Mammi Ellen replied, and her fingers fluttered up to her hair, tucking a couple of invisible strands back under her neat *kapp*. "I'd asked him to come for some pie this afternoon."

Mammi Ellen and Moe made their own plans, and as often as not, Sarai would return from an errand to find the couple sitting in the kitchen together, chatting happily about old times or working on some chore together—two being much more efficient than one. A few times, Sarai had gone out for the day and come home to find large chores completed by the two old people together. On their own, they struggled. But together, they were still able to get things done. That had been the beginning of Sarai's idea of how to make sure her grandmother would be cared for, happy and not even the faintest bit lonely if Sarai spread her wings.

"He's got someone with him today," Sarai replied, watching the old man and the younger one loping along beside to catch up. He was tall and had broad shoulders, but his head was down so she couldn't see his face under the brim of his straw hat.

"That would be Arden," Mammi said.

Sarai leaned closer to the window to get a better look. Moe's grandson Arden had moved from the community of Redemption, Pennsylvania, to Ohio a few years ago with his family. The last time she'd seen Arden, he was about eighteen and breaking hearts all over the community. He'd always been too handsome for his own good…or the good of half the girls his age.

But Arden wasn't her worry, and Sarai had bigger eggs to fry, as she liked to say.

"I don't know why you and Moe don't get married," Sarai said, casting her grandmother a smile. "You get along so well."

"Friends tend to get along," Mammi Ellen said with a chuckle. "Are you still on that idea, Sarai? I'm not looking to get married again, dear. I have great-grandchildren, white hair and arthritis. I've lived my life. If you want to worry about a wedding, make it your own."

"Setting people up is a far sight easier than finding a husband myself," Sarai replied. "Besides, Adel Knussli is keeping me in mind for her matchmaking efforts. So you don't need to worry about me."

And Shipshewana would have all sorts of people she'd never met.

"Keeping you in mind is different than rolling up her sleeves and making you her central effort," her grandmother replied. "You might think about asking Adel to do just that. You're a beautiful girl, you're smart, and you have good character. You'll make any man a lovely wife."

"Any man…" Sarai shook her head. "He'll have to be the right one, Mammi."

Because Sarai had a theory—and it was only a theory—but she didn't want to waste fifty to seventy years of her life with a man who Gott hadn't created for her especially. There were couples who seemed to be so perfectly matched that she had no doubt that Gott had placed them together like two puzzle pieces. And then there were others who were less well matched and much less happy together. If Sarai was going to vow the rest of her life to a man, then she wanted Gott's perfect will—the one right man. And who knew where Gott had him waiting?

"There is such a thing as being too careful, Sarai," Mammi Ellen said.

"Aha!" Sarai said with a laugh. "I could say the same to you, Mammi. My husband will come along in due time, but I really think there is something special there between you and Moe. My *mamm* agrees with me, you know. So it isn't only me who sees it."

"Oh, Sarai," she said and chuckled.

"You have lots of life left in you, Mammi," Sarai said. "And I see the way you brighten up when Moe is on his way over. You both do. Moe is a happier man when he's in your company."

"I can be positively delightful without marrying him," her grandmother replied. "And why do you assume that he wants anything else from me besides a piece of pie and a listening ear?"

A knock spared Sarai from having to answer, and she headed over to open the door. Moe stood there on the porch, a smile on his lined face and his grandson standing behind him. Arden had matured, deepened. Those boyish good looks had solidified into a taller, broader, more chiseled man. His face was cleanly shaved along a strong jawline, and his dark, wavy hair poked out from under his hat—time for a trim. Sarai met his direct brown gaze, and he gave her a nod.

Goose bumps ran up her arms. He'd always been a young man who had that effect, and he'd spent his *Rum-*

springa breaking hearts. But that was a long time ago, and Sarai was a grown woman now. There would be no games with the likes of Arden Stoltzfus.

"Hello, Sarai," Moe said with a smile. "You remember my grandson, I'm sure. He's come by for a visit."

Arden shot a veiled look at his grandfather, but he recovered quickly and smiled at Sarai.

"It's been a while," Arden said.

"*Yah.* A few years," she agreed. "Come on in."

The men entered, and Moe ambled directly to his usual spot at the kitchen table. Mammi Ellen shot him a smile and brought a freshly baked cherry pie to the table.

"It looks wonderful, Ellen," Moe said. "You make a fine pie. I've been looking forward to this all day."

"Oh, you're quite the sweet-talker, Moe," Mammi Ellen said with a chuckle. "But it helps to have someone to bake for, for sure and certain. Sarai and I just can't eat all the baking ourselves..."

The older folks settled into a chat, and Mammi put a pile of four plates on the table and started dishing a piece for Moe. When everyone had a slice, Mammi Ellen and Moe continued their conversation, and Sarai and Arden stood by the far kitchen window, their plates balanced in their hands.

"So what really brings you back?" Sarai asked.

"What do you mean?" Arden asked. He took a bite of pie. "Wow. This is really good. Dawdie was right."

"Don't you try and change the subject," Sarai replied. "I saw the look you gave him when he said you were here for a visit. You are not here for a visit—that was plain."

And it likely wasn't her business, either, but Sarai looked up and met his gaze all the same. "Are you moving back or something?"

Arden shook his head and lowered his voice. "I'm trying to convince my grandfather to move to Ohio to be with the rest of the family."

"Move?" Sarai frowned. "But he's so happy here."

"He's too old to take care of things on his own," Arden said.

"Oh, that's silly," Sarai said. "He knows where to come for pie, and he's very spry for his age."

"He got a bad cold this last spring," Arden said.

"I know. We helped care for him."

It had been tough for the old man. His cough lasted weeks, but they'd made him chicken soup and insisted he stay inside next to the woodstove. Sarai had changed all his linens every three days and washed everything up for him. It had been a lot of work until one of Moe's married granddaughters arrived to take over. But that was what neighbors did. Besides, Moe was special.

"We appreciate all you did to help him when he was ill," Arden said, his voice firm. "But it should be family doing it, and we shouldn't have to take a bus in order to do our duty by our grandfather, either."

"It was your sister who did it," Sarai countered.

"Last time," he agreed. "And this time—I'm here."

His words were strong, and she felt the line being drawn. He was here for his grandfather on family business, and Sarai was not family. She looked back to the kitchen table, where the old people sat eating together. Mammi was in the middle of a story, and Moe chuckled along as she talked.

"If you treat him like he's old, he'll feel old," Sarai said, turning back to Arden. "Don't you see how happy he is with Mammi Ellen?"

"*Yah*. Of course," he replied.

"I think the two of them should get married," she said, and Arden coughed and sputtered, and his face went red. "Sorry…"

She winced and waited while he coughed a few times.

"Are you all right?" Mammi Ellen asked from the table. She rose to her feet. "Let me get you some water, Arden."

Mammi went to the sink for a glass of water, and Arden accepted it with a strained smile of thanks. He drained the glass of water and cleared his throat another couple of times as Mammi went back to the table.

Arden lowered his voice. "You want to set up our grandparents?"

"It's a good idea," Sarai said. "They make each other happy. They've been good friends for years, and your *dawdie* comes over here every day for a piece of pie or a bowl of soup or sometimes just a cup of coffee. They always find something to chat about, and they're happier together."

"He's eighty-two," Arden said flatly.

"And she's seventy-eight. I don't see the problem," Sarai replied. "They're adults."

"I've been asked by my father and my uncles to come bring Dawdie home," Arden replied.

Yes, his male relatives' authority was all on his side, but Sarai saw something none of the rest saw: the way Moe and Ellen lit up when they were in the same room together. They cared deeply for each other, and Sarai thought their friendship was particularly beautiful. She took another bite of pie and chewed thoughtfully.

"It would be easier for both of them if they lived together and cared for each other," Sarai said, spearing the last bite onto her fork. "And they can't do that if they aren't married. But just look at them…"

Mammi Ellen was leaning forward, nodding and listening to Moe talk about something that Sarai couldn't make out. The happiness at being together was evident—to her, at least.

"You live with your grandmother, though," Arden countered.

"I do," she agreed. "But I won't always."

Who knew what was waiting for Sarai around the corner?

"Is someone courting you?" Arden asked.

"That's a brazen question." It was also a question that stung a little bit.

"I was just…" His face colored. "Sorry, I was curious. I thought someone would be… I mean…"

His embarrassment softened her. "No, I don't have anyone special at the moment, not that it's your business. But we do have a quality matchmaker here in Redemption, and as my *mammi* points out, I've got some marriageable qualities. So I don't think it's being too prideful to expect to find a husband."

Besides, Sarai had faith that Gott would bring the right man along…hopefully soon, and very possibly in Shipshewana.

"You'll have no problem at all." Arden shot her a lopsided smile that made her breath catch. He'd always been a charmer.

Arden had also always irritated her. While the other girls in Redemption swooned at his smiles and got their hearts broken by this too-smooth, too-handsome man, Sarai had seen him for what he was—selfish. He didn't care about the girls he disappointed. It was a game for him, and she refused to ever fall for the likes of Arden Stoltzfus. And now he'd be calling the shots for his Dawdie Moe. It wasn't right. He had no sensitivity to hearts and feelings.

"But it's not going to work to set up our grand-parents," Arden said, turning back. "Dawdie has got to come back with me to Ohio. There's no way around it."

No way, indeed. Moe might be elderly, but he was a man who could make his own choices.

"I disagree," Sarai said simply.

"You…can't. This is from his family," Arden said.

"My opinion might not mean a thing when it comes down to it," she replied with a shrug, "but I disagree with you. You were always a little too focused on yourself, and you never did look too long at the people around you. Your Dawdie Moe and my Mammi Ellen have a special friendship, and their happiness together matters, too. So you go right ahead and do what you have to. I'm determined to see those two married."

Arden looked at her, waiting to see a sign of joking, but there was none. Maybe he shouldn't be so surprised. He wasn't proud of the way he'd behaved when he'd lived here in Redemption, and it stood to reason the community here would have less respect for him after all of that. He'd made mistakes in his adolescence here—more than most people knew about. Or did Sarai guess? There was something knowing in the way she looked at him. He remembered her as the girl he simply couldn't impress. She'd been beautiful with honey-blond hair and bright blue eyes, and she'd been wise to most of his antics back then, which was just as well.

"Are you serious?" Arden asked, keeping his voice low. "Or are you teasing me?"

She'd always been beautiful enough that she could have strung out the male hearts here in Redemption, but she'd chosen not to. Staring him down now, she still looked stubbornly honest.

"I'm completely serious." Sarai met his gaze easily, not a hint of humor in her clear eyes.

"You want to set our grandparents up—arrange a marriage," he said.

"The short answer to that is *yes*," she replied.

Arden rubbed his hand over his eyes. "And if I completely disagree with you, that's going to mean nothing to you, is it?"

"I'm sorry, Arden. You don't live here. You don't see them together."

Of course. Sarai always had been a young woman with her own ideas.

"Look, Sarai, here's the thing. I have two weeks to get my grandfather packed up and ready to go with me…if I can convince him. I don't have a lot of family left in town to ask to help me, and I didn't keep in touch with many friends when I left." He paused uncertainly. "And since you and your grandmother are such close friends with my grandfather, I was going to ask if you'd help us."

"Help him leave," Sarai said.

"Help him go home to his family," Arden said.

Sarai sighed. "I do understand that you're trying to take care of him and do the right thing, Arden, but I don't want to see Moe go."

Arden nodded. "I know."

"But I suppose we can help…if, and only if, he says he wants to go with you. Then I'll be a good neighbor and help."

"I can't very well pick him up and carry him away if he isn't willing to go," Arden agreed.

"And I do have to warn you, I'll be doing my best to point out to him what a special connection our grandparents share. I'm not giving up on that."

He thought about that for a moment, but there really wasn't a way around it. "Okay. But since we're both helping out grandparents right now, and since they seem to spend a lot of time together, we might be able to work together."

"That's fair," she said.

He looked at the old people sitting at the table together. Dawdie Moe laughed softly, and Mammi Ellen had a twinkle in her eye. She seemed to feel his scrutiny, because Mammi Ellen glanced up at Arden with an expectant gaze.

"More pie, dear?" she asked.

"No, thanks," he replied. "It was delicious, though."

He held his plate and fork balanced in one hand.

"I told you that Ellen makes the best pie in Redemption, didn't I?" his grandfather asked, turning to look at Arden. "I was not exaggerating facts, was I?"

"Not a bit," Arden said. "The absolute best."

His grandfather turned back to Mammi Ellen again

and started to tell her a humorous story about selling off extra hay bales. Mammi Ellen laughed and shook her head. Arden had heard that story a hundred times already, and he could only imagine that Mammi had heard it at least once before.

"That's not quite how it happened, Moe," Ellen said. "I remember. That was after my Valentina was born…"

Sarai took his empty plate from his hand, stacked it on top of her own and headed toward the sink. An array of eggs lay over the counter on a fluffy yellow towel. They sold eggs here—he knew that much. He slipped past the dining table and into the kitchen, where Sarai stood drying her hands on a dish towel.

Sarai hadn't seemed happy to see him when he'd arrived at their door. Not that he expected a joyful greeting or anything, but he did wonder how many of his past mistakes she remembered.

He crossed the kitchen and stopped by the counter.

"Sarai, I know I was a foolish teenager," he began.

"You were a thoughtless, flirtatious young man who left girls in tears in your wake." She hung up the towel. "I had more than one friend who thought you'd been serious about her, I'll have you know. My own cousin Lizzie Peachy truly believed you'd propose to her."

Arden swallowed. "I…was a foolish young man."

"Some might say you were a liar," she said.

"Some might." He couldn't deny his bad behavior. He had one particular mistake he wanted to try to make up for on this visit, if he could. Arden owed Sarai's father some money, although he didn't know it. Arden would have to both confess his mistake and make it better, just as soon as he could summon up the courage and go empty his bank account. "Sarai, I'm not proud of how I acted back then."

"I should hope not." Still no softening in her face.

"And I'm sorry if I hurt your friends. I'd hoped they'd seen through my act… You sure did."

"I did, for sure and certain," she replied. "But too many other girls thought you were serious. Both of the girls I'm thinking of are married today, so at least you didn't do any irreparable harm."

"Good." And he meant that. He'd have hated it if he'd ruined some girl's chance at a happy marriage because he'd discovered that he was attractive to the girls and had figured out how to make them blush and trail after him. "So the plan to set up our grandparents isn't to get back at me?"

"If my plan works," she said simply, "we'll be family. So no, this is not revenge, and I'm surprised you'd think me capable of that."

Great, so now he'd offended her, too. Looking into her upturned face, those blue eyes sharp and wary, he couldn't help but notice just how beautiful she was— especially when she had her back up.

"My *dawdie* will decide what to do," he said. "Let's agree not to put any undue pressure on him, okay? That isn't fair to an old man."

"I would never do that," Sarai replied. "You catch more flies with honey than vinegar. How long are you here?"

"As long as it takes to convince my grandfather to come home with me," he said, then shrugged. "Or two weeks. Whichever comes first. I have a job to get back to."

And not only would his boss not allow him any more

time off, but Arden needed the money badly. His family had struggled since their move to Ohio, and his income kept the farm afloat.

"Okay," she said. "But if by the time you have to leave your grandfather wants to stay, then you'll allow it."

"Me? *Yah*. My *daet*? I don't know. But I'll leave without him if it's what my *dawdie* wants."

"Good. That's fair." She nodded as if they'd shaken on a deal, and she picked up a light pink egg, turned it over in her hand, then put it into a carton, completing a pattern of dark copper and light pink eggs. She shut the carton and added it to a pile.

"You might as well go sit down at the table," Sarai said. "I'll get some coffee on."

She turned then and started to bustle about with the coffee percolator and a bag of grinds. He watched her for a moment, then turned back to the table as she had told him to do. He'd come to see his grandfather, but in the back of his mind was his other obligation this visit—to finally settle his own conscience about a wrong he'd done to Sarai's father.

So Arden pulled out a chair and sat down. Sarai might want Moe and Ellen to get married, but when two elderly people without any more income wished to wed, it would involve financial support, and the Stoltzfus family didn't have the means for that.

"There was another time we lost the whole harvest." His grandfather's voice tugged his attention back to the table.

"Yah, yah…" Mammi Ellen said with a slow nod. "That was a very hard year. We lost half of ours. It took the community pulling together to keep our families fed

that winter, and we lived off our gardens exclusively all the next summer. Remember?"

"But Gott provided in the form of good neighbors," Dawdie Moe replied. "You know, Gott created us for community. I know we say that over and over again, but the longer I live, the more I know it to be true. Gott created Eve with Adam, and He created animals with their mates. He went down to the garden to walk and talk with them. We were created with a longing to connect with each other, and all too often we see hardship as misery instead of the invitation to pull closer to our friends and community."

"True, true…" Mammi Ellen murmured.

"Don't you agree, Arden?" his grandfather asked.

"Of course, Dawdie. We all need each other."

What was his grandfather getting at? Did he think Arden didn't fully appreciate his grandfather's neighbors, or was that recognition that he needed his own family in his old age now more than ever? He wished he knew, but Dawdie could be a little opaque when he wanted to be.

"Oh, that reminds me," Dawdie Moe said. "I've got the vet coming to check out my horse's stomach, so I'd best get back. I'm sorry to have to eat and run like this, Ellen."

"Well, now, what can you do?" Ellen asked with a smile. "I hope your horse's belly is okay."

"Thank you. So do I," Moe said, pushing himself to his feet. "I'll see you later, then."

"*Yah, yah.* I'll see you, Moe," Ellen replied. "So nice to see you again, Arden, all grown up."

"Thank you, Mammi Ellen." Funny how an old lady's

warm words could erase eight years just like that. He might as well be a teenage boy again.

Arden looked over his shoulder and found Sarai's gaze locked on him, her lips pursed in thought. Sarai had never been one to fall for his charms, but her intelligent, thoughtful gaze made him nervous. It was like she could see straight through him and knew how to beat him in one move.

But family had duty, too, and it was time for them to do theirs.

Chapter Two

Later that afternoon, Sarai finished sorting the eggs into various cartons. The last dozen of various patterns and colors that didn't quite make an attractive pattern in a carton she left in the mesh bowl on the counter for use in their own baking.

Outside, the trees were waving in a strong wind, and she watched a twig fly past.

"Wow," she murmured.

They'd already sold half the eggs today, and she had some set aside for special orders to be picked up in the morning. Colorful eggs laid by specialty hens were beautiful on the outside, but they were just regular on the inside. An omelet made from plain white or brown eggs tasted the same as those that came from pink, blue, green or copper shells. Inside, they were all the same, but the different-hued exteriors—the part they discarded when cooking—allowed Sarai and Mammi Ellen to sell those for double the regular price.

They reminded her of Arden all those years ago. He'd been very handsome, very charming, and the part that mattered most—the inside of him—hadn't been anything special. In fact, a boy who'd play those games with several girls at once wasn't someone Sarai could respect on any level. And why had the girls trailed after him like a line of silly ducklings? Because he was handsome, and he had a smile that could make a girl's stomach drop just by being caught in its rays. But what use was any of that if a man didn't have character as strong as his muscles?

"That Arden Stoltzfus has grown into quite a strapping man, hasn't he?" Mammi said, coming back into the kitchen with her knitting in hand.

"*Yah*, I suppose he has," Sarai replied.

"And he seemed to be talking to you very earnestly."

Sarai smiled at that. "It wasn't quite what it looked like."

"I'm not blind yet, my dear girl," Mammi said with a chuckle. "Not blind yet!"

"Don't you remember him from his *Rumspringa*?" Sarai asked.

"Most boys go a little wild during their *Rumspringas*," Mammi replied.

"So it's a free pass to act like he did?" Sarai shook her head. "I think the freedom gives us a peek into a man's real character when he's given permission to loosen up and explore."

"If I recall, there were all sorts of girls in love with him that year," Mammi replied.

"He led them on," Sarai said. "And he was absolutely shameless about it. Do you remember how Lizzie cried for days over him? He'd told her that he couldn't imagine being with any girl but her. And the next day he was telling Abigail Strauss the very same thing. And yes, you can blame the girls for being silly enough to believe him, but I personally blame him. Believing someone isn't half so reprehensible as outright lying, now, is it?"

"It was poor behavior, to be sure," Mammi agreed.

"And I don't think people change all that much," Sarai went on. "Naomi Peachy—Naomi Klassen now— was a fantastic cook ever since she was a girl. Haddie Ebersole was always strong and honest. Verna Kauffman has been the same faithful woman she always was from her teen years on up. I remember when Verna used to stop the Englishers from taking pictures of me. She was so loyal to our Amish way, and she still is. And as for me—have I changed so much since I was seventeen? No, I think that a *Rumspringa* often shows us exactly what a character is made of, Mammi. And we should believe it when someone shows us the truth of himself."

"I know why you're so cautious, Sarai," Mammi said quietly. "I do understand. Your cousin Lizzie's marriage has been difficult for her. Not every marriage is like that, and even hers won't stay that way every day of her life. People grow and change, and Lizzie and Paul will work through these rough patches and come out the other side of it better people."

"Lizzie seems to want that," Sarai said. "But Paul doesn't seem to."

"Paul is trying to appear stronger than he is. Marriage is long, and things change. Mark my words."

Yah, Sarai was a little spooked by her cousin's hasty and regrettable marriage. The problem seemed to be that Lizzie had a certain type of man she had been drawn to. Paul was just like Arden. He'd been bold and flirtatious, with the confidence of a bull. And where had that gotten her cousin? She was now married to a man who flirted with women, sometimes right in front of her. Yet he didn't seem to show Lizzie that she was precious to him anymore. Now that he'd married her, he took her for granted. He was selfish and wanted things his way all the time, and Lizzie was well and truly stuck with him.

If Lizzie could go back in time, Sarai had a feeling that she wouldn't have married Paul after all. But there was no way but forward, and Lizzie would have to live with her choice. But that wasn't what Sarai wanted to talk about.

"Did you know that Arden has come to take Moe back to Ohio with him?" Sarai asked.

Mammi Ellen froze. "What?"

Sarai hadn't quite meant to announce it like that. "I know. I was upset about it, too. But he says he's here from Ohio to bring his grandfather home with him. He says Moe is getting too old to take care of himself anymore, and they want him to go be with family."

"Oh, dear..." Mammi sighed. "I know he's getting older, but then, so am I. I didn't realize it was so bad. Did he tell them it was time?"

"No. From what I understand, Arden is here to convince him."

"Oh." Mammi's eyebrows went up. "Is he, now?"

Mammi headed over to the sink. She turned on the water, but her gaze was fixed out the window, and she did nothing with the running tap.

"Are you all right, Mammi?"

Her grandmother picked up a water glass and filled it, then turned the water off. "*Yah*, I'm fine, dear."

"You'll miss him if he goes, won't you?"

"I'll miss him a great deal." Mammi looked at the glass of water and placed it untouched on the counter.

"He doesn't have to go," Sarai said.

"If his family is asking him to come, and at his age…"

"He's only a few years older than you, Mammi, and I don't see you moving in with anyone just yet," Sarai replied.

"In all fairness, I have you living with me, my dear girl."

"But Moe is still strong, and he comes over here every day," Sarai pressed. "He takes care of his farm, and he has you. Unless someone is looking to get their hands on the farm early, I don't see why he should be pushed out."

"You don't think—" Mammi stopped, worry swimming in her blue eyes.

"Who inherits the place?" Sarai's mind was clicking forward, trying to figure out the problem. When an elderly person went to live with a son or daughter, the land would go to whoever was meant to inherit it, and they would begin running the farm.

"I don't know." Mammi shook her head. "But that would be wicked indeed to push an old man off his own farm in order to take over!"

"I don't know what's happening," Sarai said. "All I know is that Moe is perfectly fine where he is, and Arden has been sent here to bring Moe back to Ohio with him."

Was Arden set to inherit? Or was his father, and

Arden was simply sent to do the dirty work of bringing Dawdie home? Sarai knew that the Stoltzfus family in Ohio weren't well-off. That was common knowledge.

"Sarai, I know that look on your face. Don't jump to conclusions," Mammi Ellen said.

"You have me here to help you with housework and cooking and outdoor work," Sarai said. "But I do more than that. I'm here if someone tries to take advantage of you or pressure you into something you don't want to do. Moe doesn't have that right now. He's on his own over there, and I have a sneaking suspicion that if Moe leaves, someone will benefit. It isn't right to let poor Moe be pressured into something he doesn't want to do, even if the family's intentions are completely pure."

"No, it isn't…" Mammi pressed her lips together. "Let's pray on it."

At least Mammi could see the problem. If Arden whisked Moe back to Ohio, not only would he miss out on his dear old farm, but there would be no more time for Mammi Ellen and Moe to discover that they were truly meant to be together.

When Sarai went to bed that night, she prayed for Gott to intervene. She prayed for Him to show Moe and Mammi just what happiness they could have together, and she prayed for Him to turn Arden's mind away from taking his grandfather away…somehow! She prayed very specifically, and while she knew that Gott's ways were not her ways, and His mind was not her mind, she did believe that He was working, even when they didn't see it. And so she prayed all the same.

She lay in her bed for a long time, her gaze focused on the ceiling. She'd come to stay with her grandmother because there was no one else to do it. Her older sisters were married with children of their own, and her brother had moved to another community for a job at a factory that paid very well. Everyone's life had started…her cousins, her siblings… They'd all gone on their own adventures or gotten married and had homes of their own. It was difficult being the unmarried one, always feeling like she was waiting for her life to start.

When she closed her eyes, she imagined in her mind's eye a chance at starting fresh in Shipshewana. It would include growing a flock of specialty hens and meeting new people. And maybe there would be a man who would be so good, so honest, so well spoken of, that she wouldn't feel any fear at all at the thought of taking her lifelong vows and starting the rest of her life…

She couldn't imagine what he'd look like. His face was a blur. But he'd be tall and strong, she was certain, with a straw hat he'd wear perfectly straight on his head.

After Sarai drifted off to sleep, the wind started. There wasn't a drop of rain, but a gale began to blow. It howled around the chicken coops, and it whistled over the stable roof. Trees thrashed, and as Sarai slept that night, she dreamed of tornadoes, even though the closest she'd ever been to one was seeing it on a TV screen in a store in town. And when she woke up the next morning, the storm had stopped, but outside the window, strewed across the yard in the rose-gold sunlight, there were twigs and small branches, garden signs for cabbage and onions that must have blown over from the neighbors.

Sarai got dressed and went downstairs. Mammi was up already, stoking the fire in the big woodstove on the cooking porch.

"What on earth happened last night?" Sarai asked.

"Didn't you hear it?" Mammi asked.

"I didn't hear anything!"

"It was a windstorm," Mammi said. "It was short but powerful. We have a lot of cleaning up to do."

Mammi looked forlornly out over the backyard. It was then that Sarai saw the worst of the damage. One chicken coop had lost its roof entirely, and the other had most of the shingles stripped right off. The chickens scratched in the dirt, clucking softly to each other.

"Did we lose any hens?" Sarai gasped, rushing past her grandmother, off the porch and into the grass. She looked around the hen yard, mentally counting the birds by twos.

"I believe they are all still there," Mammi called back. "Much like Paul and Silas in the prison—everything shook, the doors flew open, and they stayed put."

And while Sarai was grateful that the hens were all there, her stomach dropped at the sight of all the work awaiting them.

Perhaps Sarai's prayers last night had been too specific, too proud, too certain that she knew what was right, and Gott was showing her how little control over things she really had.

I'm sorry if I was presumptuous, Gott, she silently prayed. *I'll just ask that You give us the strength to do the work in front of us.*

This morning, in the face of the windstorm damage, that seemed like a safer prayer.

Arden washed his hands in the mudroom sink, letting the soap foam up through his fingers. He'd tidied up the stable. It was evident that someone had been helping his grandfather get the outdoor work done, but they weren't coming half often enough. Giving the stable a proper cleaning had taken him two hours longer than it should have.

"I've got the oatmeal ready, Arden!" Dawdie called from the kitchen. "And I've got fresh blueberries to go on top, too."

"Thank you, Dawdie. I'll be right there."

Arden rinsed and dried his hands, then headed into the kitchen, where his grandfather waited for him. The oatmeal was on the table, and his grandfather had a towel tied around his middle. Not an apron—those were for women—but definitely a makeshift covering to protect his clothing. His grandfather untied the baling twine he'd used to hold the towel in place and dropped his contraption on an unused chair.

"It's nice to have a young man around here again," Dawdie said. "Sit. Let's pray."

Arden pulled out a chair in front of an empty bowl and spoon, and he bowed his head in silent prayer. When his grandfather cleared his throat, the prayer was over.

"That was a strong wind last night," Dawdie said. "Any damage in the stable?"

The old man leaned forward and dished a scoop of oatmeal into Arden's bowl for him.

"A little bit," Arden said. "Some shingles came off on the east side of the roof. I'll help you get that fixed up today."

"That's nice of you," Dawdie said. His hands stayed busy with serving himself as he talked. "Someone will come by and check on me, though, Arden. You can be sure of that. The church hasn't forgotten me."

"*Yah, yah*, I know," Arden replied. "But we miss you. My *daet* tells us stories about you all the time. I think he misses you a lot. And you know my *daet*—he doesn't like to show his feelings. But they're there."

"What stories does he tell about me?" Dawdie asked.

"Oh, about how you used to take him fishing, and how you got frostbite on your nose one year when you were harvesting ice. He talks about your makeshift aprons, too."

"It isn't an apron," Moe replied. "It just protects my shirts. Otherwise, I'd be doing more laundry, and who has time for that?"

There was fresh, creamy milk and the promised bowl of fresh wild blueberries. How long his grandfather had spent gathering them that morning, he didn't know. There were a few leaves in the bowl, and Arden pulled them out and put them on the table before sprinkling some berries onto his oatmeal.

"Who does your laundry, Dawdie?" Arden asked, taking a bite. The oatmeal was well cooked, and he was hungry after a morning of hard work.

"Well, there's a lady who used to come by every Saturday, and she'd include my clothes in her Monday wash. But then I started helping Ellen next door on wash day, and we just did our wash together."

"Helping Ellen with the wash…how?" Arden asked. Because that was decidedly a woman's chore, and he had trouble imagining his grandfather doing it.

"Well…just helping. I carry the basket, and she feeds the clothes into the wringer washer. And she'll hand me wet clothes, and I'll put them on the line. Then we bring it all back in together. It doesn't take as long for her with another set of hands. But then her granddaughter arrived, and we couldn't very well carry on like that, could we?"

"So who does it for you now?" Arden asked.

"Sarai."

That beautiful woman who eyed him as if she were weighing him on her own personal scales was the one to do his grandfather's laundry. It was more appropriate than his arrangement with Ellen, but he still wasn't sure he liked it.

Arden tried to sound neutral. "Right. Well, it's a lot of work for one woman to do, I imagine."

"She's a great help to Ellen. A great help. Besides, I pitch in, too."

"Yah?" Arden asked.

"I have a man who brings me steaks, and I always share with Ellen and Sarai," Dawdie said. "I don't eat that much anymore at my age. I can only eat half a steak on a good day. And I've helped Ellen sort out her horse tack more times than I can count. We're neighbors. We help each other."

"I'm not suggesting that you are a burden on anyone, Dawdie, but you're getting older, and we're your family. It's only right you come be with us," Arden said.

That was what his *daet* had been saying, and Aunt Hazel, and Uncle Herm, and everyone else in the family who'd settled out in Ohio. It was time. He was their father, and it was time to come be together as was proper.

"I raised your *daet* in this very house, you know," Dawdie said. He pointed across the table. "He used to sit at the corner of the table between his sister and brother, right there. That was his spot. The *kinner* used to like to play tricks on me when I came home for dinner, and they'd scoot around and change chairs and giggle as if it was the biggest joke." Dawdie chuckled. "And your *mammi* always saved me a chicken leg. Always. She'd bring the platter to the table, and she'd take the leg and put it on my plate and say, 'That's for Daet.'"

Dawdie smiled and looked around the room as if he could almost see those giggling *kinner* and his lovely wife... He fell silent. Then he took a bite of oatmeal.

"You love this house," Arden said quietly.

"*Yah.* I do. But I love you all, too. There are memories here of a different time, when I was Daet, and everyone was so excited when I came home. My wife was beautiful, and my children always had too much energy, and it seemed like we'd be like that forever."

Arden wasn't sure how to answer. He'd heard some friends talk about their young children in a similar way, but Arden didn't have a wife and children. Not yet. He'd changed his mind about the kind of woman he wanted, and he was no longer sure about how to win over a girl like that. They ate in silence for a couple of minutes, and Arden dished himself up a second bowl.

"You have grandchildren in Ohio," Arden pointed out. Arden was one of them.

"*Yah*, that I do. I love seeing you, too, Arden. But leaving the house that has been home since I was a newly married man...that's harder than you think. You'll understand when you get married and have some little ones of your own." Dawdie put his spoon down. "Whatever happened with that young lady you were spending time with? Your parents thought it might be serious."

It had been serious. He'd started to prepare his family for an engagement announcement.

"Mary." Arden felt his throat tighten. "It didn't work out."

"Why not?"

"She wanted a richer man than I am," Arden said. When she'd figured out how tight his finances were, she'd cooled off.

"Richer?" Dawdie made a face. "You've got a good job."

"*Yah*, and she was very close to agreeing to marry me. It was almost set. Then someone's nephew from Pennsylvania here came to visit, and she was suddenly very busy. She had no time for me. They announced their engagement in a matter of weeks."

"Oh, Arden…" Dawdie sighed. "I'm sorry. I didn't know it was like that."

Arden wasn't sure what to say, and he turned his attention to eating again.

"Are you looking for a wife?" Dawdie asked. "Because we have a matchmaker here now. Adel Draschel, whose husband Mark died—do you remember them?"

"*Yah*," he replied. "He was a deacon."

"*Yah*, well, she remarried—Jacob Knussli—and she's been standing as matchmaker for a while now. She's had some good success. If you want me to introduce you—"

"No, Dawdie. I'm not here to find a wife. I'm here to bring you home," Arden said with a wry smile. "I will find a wife, but I have to figure out how to find the right kind of girl first. That's the hard part."

"It is, I agree." His grandfather pushed himself to his feet and carried his bowl to the sink. He leaned forward to look out the back window and frowned.

"What's wrong?" Arden asked.

"The wind really did some damage next door," Moe said. "I can't see too well from here, but it looks like one coop is missing a roof!"

"What?" Arden stood up and went to the window next to his grandfather. He leaned forward to get a better look, and his grandfather was right. The stable next door was missing shingles, too, and there were limbs and leaves and even what looked like a large sheet of plastic strewed across the yard. "They got the worst of it."

"Poor Ellen," Moe said softly. "She obviously can't do all that herself. We'll have to go over and help."

"Yah…" Arden couldn't see any other way around it, either. But there was a wriggle of worry in his gut, too. Sarai had all but informed him that she was going to do her best to set up the old people.

How vulnerable was his grandfather to this sort of thing? He'd need to be protected so that he could come home and be with his family. Those rambunctious children who used to surround his table were all grown now, with *kinner* of their own. And they needed Dawdie Moe in their lives, too.

"Dawdie, of course we'll help, but—" Arden began.

"But?" Dawdie turned, suddenly filled with more energy. "But what?"

How was he supposed to bring up that Sarai had other plans for the old man?

"Nothing," he said. "Let's clean up and head over."

"Yah, let's do that." His grandfather headed back to

the table and began to clear it. "A woman can't be left on her own to clean up after a storm like that. That's why there's men's work and there's women's work. She's a good woman, that Ellen. She's kind and decent. And she makes the best pie I've ever had."

"What about Mammi?" Arden asked. His grandfather's late wife.

"Your grandmother made the best strudel, and she wouldn't have been jealous at all to know that another woman bested her pies. She knew her strudel couldn't be beaten. But Ellen has been having a hard time lately. She's had one thing after another go wrong. It started with her wringer washer popping a leak, and then some fool teenagers in a pickup truck knocked her egg sign right over... One thing after another, and I've been doing my best to help her out. It's just been a spell of difficulties."

Dawdie bustled over to the icebox and put the milk back. He was more lively now, and Arden helped to clear the rest of the table. His grandfather did seem to get more energized when he talked about Ellen. He seemed more determined, more sure of himself. Was Sarai right? Was there something budding between their grandparents?

"Dawdie, are you courting Ellen?" Arden asked.

"What?" Moe stopped short, and color suffused his cheeks above his white beard. "No. No, of course not. I'm her friend. We've known each other for years. We've helped each other out more times than I can count. And now it's my turn to help her. We'll get her property cleaned up and anything else that needs fixing. And I won't be leaving that to the rest of the community. I'm her neighbor, Arden. Around here, that means something."

Arden nodded. "Of course, Dawdie. I was just wondering if maybe there was something more than friendship between you."

"A man doesn't help a woman only in return for her romantic affections," Moe retorted. "That's not right, is it? You help because women aren't as strong, and Gott gave us men muscles for a reason. That's why. In fact, young man, I think you could learn that lesson. Helping a woman in her time of need isn't about charming her or flirting with her. It's about being a good and decent man."

In his eighties, Dawdie Moe didn't quite have the muscular physique of a younger man, but Arden could appreciate the point. Even when a body aged, a man still felt his masculine duty.

"I'm sorry, Dawdie. I didn't mean to offend you," Arden said.

"I'm not offended." But Dawdie certainly looked a little miffed. "My neighbor matters to me. She's been a dear friend to me for years. This is what we do. You might learn a thing or two about being neighborly, Arden."

"*Yah*, I understand," Arden said quickly. "You're doing the right thing, and I'll help. Let's head over."

Because the sooner they started, the sooner they could finish up and Arden could get his grandfather to make a firm choice about going back to Ohio. It looked like Dawdie Moe needed a little more time to adjust to the idea, and Arden wasn't sure they had that.

Chapter Three

Sarai tossed a handful of feed into the chicken pen. The birds scratched at the ground, pecking at bugs, and startled when the feed fell, then turned toward it to eat. For creatures who'd had their roof ripped off the night before, they were surprisingly calm, and that was a mercy. Birds twittered from the apple trees, and the horses ambled through the pasture munching fresh grass. If it weren't for the damage, she wouldn't know anything had happened.

The missing roof to the smaller chicken coop lay several yards away with nails ominously sticking out of it. A small white butterfly landed on the tip of one of the nails and rested there, wings still for a moment before it fluttered away again.

"What a strange storm," Mammi Ellen said, and she bent down, picking up a stray shingle. "But sometimes we get them. What can you do?"

Sarai looked over her shoulder and saw Moe and Arden on their way over. Moe had picked up his pace more than usual, but it was Arden who caught her eye. He'd always been good-looking—with the kind of looks that made even Englisher girls stop and take a second look. But some handsome teenagers grew into very ordinary-looking men. That seemed to be a blessing, in a way, because they knew what it was like to make a girl blush, and then they matured and knew what it was like to work hard and not be any more special than any other man in the community.

But Arden hadn't lost his looks as he aged. He had a way of walking that seemed more like a saunter, and his gaze was like steel. She let out a shaky breath and purposely glanced away again. Arden might be fine to look at, but that didn't matter a bit when she knew the bedrock of his character.

Sarai tossed another handful of feed into the pen and then headed over to the second, smaller one that held her specialty fowl. She opened the door, and the chickens clambered over for their breakfast. The chortles and bock-bocks filled the air.

"Here's hoping the storm didn't startle them too much. I'd hate for them to be put off laying," Sarai said, raising her voice so her grandmother might hear her.

"What's that, dear?" her grandmother called back.

"I said, I hope the storm didn't scare the hens too much," she said, louder still. "I don't want them to be put off laying."

"That would be a shame." But the voice was deep, strong, and she startled, turning to see Arden come up behind her. He'd arrived faster than she expected.

"It would be," Sarai said. "But they seem calm enough. I hope that means they'll keep up their laying."

"That was a big storm last night," Arden said.

"I didn't hear it," she admitted. "I guess I slept too deeply."

"I listened to it howl half the night," Arden said. "It looks like your place got walloped worse than my grandfather's, though."

"I wish I knew why," she said, and her mind went back to her earnest, insistent prayers the night before. That was surely a coincidence, wasn't it? Gott didn't punish His children for pleading with Him, did He? Unless she'd been truly too presumptuous. But who else could she turn to if not Gott?

"You look worried," Arden said.

"No." She forced a smile.

"We came to help," Arden said. "We'll get your yard cleaned up and repair your coops…and I saw where some shingles came off your stable—we can fix that up, too."

"That's a lot of work," Sarai said.

"I thought we agreed we'd help each other with our grandparents. Fair is fair, I think. Besides, my grandfather made an eloquent point this morning about helping his neighbors."

Sarai looked over to where Moe and her grandmother stood talking. Moe had his hat pushed back on his head, and he bent down to pick up the piece of plastic tarp that had blown in. It took him a little longer to stand up straight.

"Moe is a good man," Sarai said quietly. "Really good. I mean, he's better than most."

"*Yah*, I know," Arden agreed. "And he's determined to set your grandmother's property to rights again. On his own, if he has to."

Sarai smiled faintly. "He means well."

"You can see that he needs help, can't you?" Arden asked. "He's an old man."

"If he were on his own, I'd agree," she said. "But together with my *mammi*, they do surprisingly well. They take care of dishes, cooking, cleaning out the stove… They're pretty efficient. He wraps a towel around his waist—he's got this twine he uses—"

"*Yah*, I know," Arden interrupted. "I've seen his apron."

"Don't call it that!" Sarai said. "He is very sensitive about it. But I've seen those two in the kitchen together. Mammi makes bread, and Moe washes down the counters. They do just fine together."

"What about this outdoor work?" Arden asked.

"You could pay someone to do it." It would be simple enough.

Arden's expression changed to something less confident, and he shrugged. "*Yah*, we could." He was silent for a moment. "Supporting a family isn't as easy as it looks, you know. And I've been working really hard to make a start there."

"I never said it was easy." Sarai felt some recrimination in his words. "You know, I might not have worked outside the home before, Arden, but this egg business is a real business. We have to care for the hens, clean and box up the eggs, deal with customers and orders, and manage the money. It's not just a hobby or something. The money we make keeps the hens fed and the coops in shape. We have all the eggs we need and then some. We even have a little money left over for a treat every week after we sell our eggs. We hosted a whole dinner for the extended family last week with the egg money. Plus, I'm saving for a bus ticket to see my aunt and uncle in Shipshewana. I don't need a penny from my parents."

And that was saying something. She didn't know any young, unmarried women her age who didn't need some money from their parents for their personal needs or to take a little trip. She'd done better than that.

"That's good," Arden said.

"And I'll have you know that other people have looked at this business and have seen promise in something like it for themselves," she went on. "Eggs always sell, but specialty eggs draw in a different kind of customer. The customer wants something singular, and we deliver on that."

"I'm not insulting your egg business," he said quietly.

"Good." Because it felt a bit like a head pat to her, but she wasn't some foolish girl who didn't understand how things worked. She wasn't just a woman waiting for a man to take care of things for her and not appreciating how hard that was. And if all went well with Mammi Ellen and Moe, Sarai would show her family in Shipshewana how to raise the hens.

Ellen and Moe crumpled the big tarp between them, and Moe tucked it under one arm. Then Ellen bent down to pick up some more plastic garbage and another thick black shingle.

"We can't let them work too hard," Arden said, following her gaze toward the old people. "My grandfather thinks he's younger than he is."

"I agree," Sarai said. "But how about you be the one

to tell Moe and Ellen that they're too old to be really useful. I'll watch from here."

Arden shot her a wry smile. "That wouldn't be smart of me, now, would it?"

"What do you expect to do?" she asked.

"Well, I'll do the repairs myself," Arden said. "Maybe you could keep an eye on them and stop them from doing too much."

"What do you mean, do it yourself?" she demanded. "This is my grandmother's and my home, too. I'm perfectly capable of working on it. I might not know how to reshingle a roof on my own, but I can help if you tell me what to do."

"*Yah*, okay," Arden said with a nod. "We'll work together, then. We'll fix everything up and make sure our grandparents feel like they're helping without letting them strain themselves."

Moe came up then, the tarp under his arm.

"Hi, Moe," Sarai said with a smile. "It's so nice of you to come over."

"I'm happy to come. How are you doing, Sarai?" Moe asked. "How are the chickens?"

"They seem pretty content," Sarai said, "but the laying for the next few days will tell us where they're really at. Chickens are much more sensitive than people realize."

"Especially your fancy chickens there," Moe said.

"*Yah*, especially them. We have orders for the colored eggs. I hate to disappoint customers."

"It'll be okay, Sarai," Moe said, patting her arm. "Don't you worry. Arden and I will help you two ladies get sorted out, and before you know it, everything will be running like normal."

Moe always sounded so reasonable, and Sarai felt her own tension start to dissipate.

"Do you think so?" she asked.

"Oh, of course," Moe replied. "Storms come. Wind blows. Things get damaged. If nothing ever went back to normal again, the world would be in a sorry state, wouldn't it?"

"*Yah*, it would," Sarai agreed.

"Arden, we need to get some roofing supplies," Moe said. "And I'm sure we'll have to pick up a few more things. Let's make a list."

Sarai looked over at Arden. Moe would be hard to derail once he got working, and Arden was right that his grandfather needed to work at a slower pace.

"Moe, why don't you and Mammi get something to eat?" Sarai said.

"I'm just fine. I just had breakfast," Moe replied. "I'm as spry as a steer."

"But Mammi hardly touched hers," Sarai said, lowering her voice. "And I worry sometimes that she doesn't eat or rest enough. This is a lot of work, and I'd hate to see her tired out. I'd do it myself and take her inside, but you know my Mammi Ellen. She's more stubborn than she looks."

Moe chuckled at that. "Most women are, young lady."

"And men, too," Sarai joked back. "You know her better than anyone else, Moe. And she won't listen to me, but if you asked her to go inside and rest, I know she'd listen to you."

"Oh…" Moe sobered. "Oh, my. I didn't realize that. This is men's work out here, though. She shouldn't be worrying over men's work—"

"And we can't do much until we have supplies," Arden cut in. "Why don't me and Sarai go to town and pick up those supplies, and you can make sure Ellen gets some food and off her feet for a little bit until we get back." Arden looked between them. "Does that sound good?"

"*Yah*, that works for me," Sarai agreed quickly. "Moe, is that okay for you?"

"*Yah*." Moe nodded. "You can count on me. I'll make sure she takes care of herself properly. Arden, I have tabs at the ranch supply store and the hardware store. You can just add anything you need to the tab."

"I'll go hitch up," Arden said.

"And I'll go get my purse, too," Sarai said.

Arden was right about one thing: if they were going to keep the old people from overworking themselves, they'd have to get to the heavy lifting first.

As Arden strode away, Sarai turned back to Moe.

"You're a good man, Moe," she said. "You have a wonderful instinct for taking care of women. I wonder if you haven't considered getting married again?"

"At my age?" he said with a short laugh.

Sarai shrugged. "You don't seem so old to me."

"Don't I?" Moe looked at her from the corner of his eye.

"Not at all." She cast him a brilliant smile. "Look at you coming to our rescue this way. I don't think you're old at all, Moe."

The old man's cheeks colored a little bit.

"I'd better get my things now," she said.

And Sarai walked briskly toward the house, leaving Moe with that little thought to chew over. He might need a nudge, but a few well-planted seeds just might get him to realize exactly what he had with Mammi Ellen and what he still had to give to a woman in a home.

Arden had finished hitching up the horse to the buggy when Sarai walked across the freshly mowed lawn to Moe's driveway. Arden would make sure the lawn was cut again before he left, and he'd get the gardening all done for his *dawdie*, as well. And he was hoping he'd be arranging a moving truck to transport his grandfather's personal items to Ohio, too. He was prepared to get busy—if his grandfather would let him. And if Sarai would help, too, they'd be able to get everything done.

If she'd help. She'd said she would, but he knew how little she wanted his grandfather to move.

Sarai stopped at the side of the buggy while he tightened the last strap, slipping two fingers under the leather to make sure it wasn't too tight.

"Do you remember your way around here?" Sarai asked.

"Of course I do." He shook his head. "I haven't been gone that long."

"Four years."

He mentally tallied it up. She was right. Four years.

"Well, I haven't forgotten yet. I did my growing up here." He'd done more growing up in the last two years than he'd done since his *Rumspringa*, though. But he wasn't going to admit to that. It was embarrassing. He nodded to the buggy.

"Are our grandparents taking it easy over there?" he asked.

"I think they are. They can talk for hours. We've just insisted upon it. They'll enjoy themselves."

Sarai pulled herself up and settled into the seat, and he joined her and untied the reins. There was a time when he was young and rash when he'd wanted a chance to drive with her in his buggy…but the likes of Sarai Peachy didn't go driving with boys like him. Not in that way, at least. Not back then. Probably not now, either.

He flicked the reins, and the horse started forward, wheels crunching over the gravel. A pair of bluebirds swept down in front of the buggy and landed on a tree branch overhead.

"My grandfather mentioned you in letters," he said.

"He did?"

"*Yah.* He said he was surprised you weren't married yet."

"There is a lot of pressure put on women to get married," she said. "An unfair amount of pressure."

"I don't think he meant any insult," Arden said. "He just meant that he thought you'd have lots of options."

"There have been a few," she said. "But I'm being careful."

"Why so careful?"

"It's very ironic that you'd ask me that," she countered.

"Ironic? How?" He darted her a cautious look.

"A man like you," she said. "You swept through our community, breaking hearts left and right, and then left town. You might not think about those women again, but you damaged their reputations. They looked silly for having fallen for your charms."

Arden blinked. "I…uh…" He wasn't sure what to say to that. "I'm sorry. But you never fell for my charms."

"No, I didn't," she replied. "But that was only because I was watching Lizzie and some of my other friends be made fools of by you. And I could see what you were up to."

"So you're too smart for that," he said. "Why should I hold you back?"

He turned the horse onto the road in the direction of the town of Redemption, and the buggy wheels bumped up onto the pavement for a smoother ride.

"You?" She shook her head. "You don't hold me back, Arden. But Lizzie did get married, and she found another man who was brazen and brash and very forward. And she's lived to regret that choice."

"He can't be that bad," he said. How bad did a man have to be for a woman to regret marrying him?

"He is. He's selfish. He doesn't listen to Lizzie. He wants to be right all the time. He makes foolish choices and won't take her input. He openly flirts with other women, too. I've seen her cry more often than I've seen her smile."

Lizzie Peachy had been a pretty, sweet girl. "I'm sorry it turned out that way. Who did she marry?"

"His name is Paul Swarey. He's from Bird in Hand, and she comes to visit us much more often than a happy wife would."

So no one he knew. If he'd known the man, he might have paid him a visit and told him that people were talking and he'd better shape up. But who knew what the men who'd known him even thought of him now.

"Anyway, I've been watching and learning," she went

on. "And I don't want to end up like Lizzie. I realized that it isn't just about finding someone who wants to marry you. It's about finding someone worthy of a life-long vow. That's much harder."

Sarai had always been a bit of a know-it-all, but he was noticing something now: she was scared. That was what this was. She was scared of getting married, and so she tried to be an armchair expert on the topic.

"And that's why you're single still?" he asked, softening his tone. "You're being cautious?"

"Of course I'm careful!" she said. "I know what I stand to lose if I make the wrong choice."

"Or what you stand to gain if you make the right one," he countered.

She didn't answer.

"You get quiet when I'm right," he said, but he cast her a smile to soften the words.

"Gott will bring me the right man," she said. "I believe that."

Fair enough. He'd been praying that Gott would provide him the right kind of woman, too, but he wasn't sure how to go about finding her. Anyone who knew about his youth wasn't about to risk her future with him, and the ones who'd only met him in Ohio saw a man who didn't make much money and didn't have roots in the area deep enough for them to ask around about him. The right woman was going to have to see deeper on her own.

But Sarai wasn't only a good, hardworking woman. She was also stunningly beautiful. She would have her pick of men—he knew how this worked. And she'd been well provided for all these years. Women like Sarai had expectations of their own.

Arden flicked the reins, speeding the horse up to a trot. The road was familiar; this area had a feel all its own. It was in his blood. Overhanging branches tickled the top of his buggy, leaves scraping softly overhead until they emerged onto clear road once more.

"My grandfather says you all have a matchmaker out here now," he said.

"*Yah.* Adel Knussli."

"Have you considered using her?" he asked.

"I have other plans, actually," she said.

"*Yah?* Like what?"

She eyed him for a moment. "I'm not ready to talk about it yet."

"Fine." It shouldn't matter to him, but he wished she would. He was curious about the plans a woman like her made for herself.

"I'm good at running a business, you know," she said after a moment of silence. "I have a knack for it. I can see how the money works. That sounds crass, but I can see it. I can see how expenses and income work together, and how to set things up to appeal to what people want. And it's…it's not fun, exactly…"

"No?" He glanced over at her.

"Okay, maybe it is fun," she said. "But it's more than fun. It's very satisfying. It's like when you put together one of those wooden puzzles and the pieces fall into place with that perfect click."

"That is satisfying," he agreed.

"The wife in Proverbs 31 works hard, you know," she went on. "She's smart and capable and runs businesses.

So you might say I'm not being very feminine, but I say I'm using the gifts Gott gave me."

He heard something defensive in her tone, and he'd met enough insecure men to feel like he could see exactly what had happened.

"So who told you you were being unfeminine by being better at business than him?" he asked with a small smile.

She looked over at him in surprise.

"Come on," he coaxed. "Just tell me."

"Abram Yoder." She rolled her eyes. "But don't you use that for common gossip, Arden. I shouldn't have said."

"And was he taking you out driving at the time?" he asked.

"*Yah*. But it didn't last past two drives."

What a shortsighted fool Abram Yoder was. "Was he the kind of man *you* wanted?"

"Until he told me I should focus on my cooking and leave the money to a man, I thought he was. He's got a very good roofing business, and he's serious and focused, but…"

"He didn't appreciate your skills," he finished for her.

"And I didn't feel the right connection," she replied. "I can go driving with a man, and I can tell right away if there's something special there. Or at least I think I will. So far, I haven't found it. I don't know if that's my problem, though. Because other girls fall halfway in love with a man based on a bit of flirting. I don't."

Yah, he'd learned that over the years. Plenty of girls did.

"That's a good thing that you don't," he said. "Trust me."

She shot him a mildly amused smile. "You would

know about that." That stung. "It's turning into a challenge, though. Everyone, including my grandmother, thinks I'm too careful. You probably don't know what to make of me, do you?"

"You're a decent woman," he replied. "I'm curious to see what kinds of plans you make."

"You really want to know?" she asked.

"*Yah*, if you'll tell me. I won't meddle. I live too far away for that. I'm probably a safe sounding board in that respect."

She nodded. "That's a logical point. All right, I will tell you. I want to go to my aunt and uncle in Shipshewana and help them build up their tour business. They have tourists who come through their house and see how a real Amish home runs—it's fascinating for Englishers. I suppose I'd be equally fascinated to see how they do things. But my aunt and uncle want to broaden out, and they like how I raise specialty hens. I'm good at it, but I'm also fascinated by the rest of their business. I think I could help them grow it and maybe learn how to start something up of my own."

Arden looked over at her, intrigued. "You don't see chickens in your future?"

"I'll always have chickens, I imagine, but you need a much larger chicken farm than I maintain to make a real living at it."

"Does getting married fit into that?" he asked.

"Of course. I could meet new people in Shipshewana. People who don't already know me so very well. It would be a fresh start."

That was exactly what his *daet* had told him he needed when they moved to Ohio and exactly what he was starting to appreciate now. A fresh start could be priceless.

"I know that feeling," he agreed. "I got my fresh start in Ohio. And if I can get a fresh start, anyone can."

They passed under a low-hanging branch, and a twig scraped along the roof of the buggy.

"Is your fresh start working out for you?" she asked.

"Not as well as I'd hoped, honestly. It's not like I stepped into a new community and everything came together for me. It's been really hard work, and I've gotten my heart broken. But I understand what you mean about wanting a new beginning of your own. Sometimes you need to get far from the people who know you best to get a fair chance. I could never marry a girl from Redemption. They know the worst of me. I need someone who never saw that—who only sees me now, for whatever that's worth."

Sarai turned forward, her lips pressed together in a thin line.

"You disagree," he said.

"I didn't say that."

"You didn't have to. You don't hide it well."

Sarai laughed. "All right, then. I'll just say it. Women aren't so easily fooled. A wise woman can sense when a man is hiding something."

"I'm not hiding anything," he said. "I'm the son of a struggling farmer. I work with my *daet* on the farm and try to make a substandard piece of land profitable. I don't hide any of it."

"Sure you do. You hide your history."

"It wouldn't be much of a fresh start if I dragged every one of my regrets along with me, would it?" Arden could stop here and argue the finer points of a starting over with her, but he was too close to unearthing some information that would really help him get his life moving in the right direction. "So how do I marry a good woman?"

"I don't think I can tell you that," she replied.

"It's not so easily done?" he asked.

"*Yah*, that's part of it, but the other part is that I don't think it's right to give you the secret to winning a good woman's heart. If you haven't figured it out on your own, then I don't think you're ready for it."

He chuckled. "You're joking." He looked over at her, but her expression was completely sober now. "You don't think I'm a decent man now, do you?"

"I think you are who you are," she said. That was an attempt at diplomacy.

"And who am I?" he asked.

"You're a flirt, Arden," she said with a sigh. "You know it, and I know it. You know how to make a girl feel whatever you want her to feel. And I think that's wrong."

"I also didn't know how far-reaching the consequences would be," he countered. "I flirted, but the girls liked it. And I always cut things off before it got serious. Or at least I thought I had. It felt like a game back then. A lot of us treated it like a game at that age. You can't say there weren't girls who did the exact same thing!"

"That doesn't make it right."

"I agree. It doesn't. I was foolish, but I wasn't mean on purpose. I've grown up since then. I'm not the same way anymore," he countered.

"We'll see about that." She shrugged. "Arden, I have no doubt that you'll find a woman who will soften to your charms. I don't know what you're worrying about."

And that wasn't his problem.

"I did find one," Arden said. "She used me and broke my heart. Maybe I had that coming after all the havoc I created here in Redemption. But I got my payback."

"What happened?"

He might as well tell her. Everyone back in Ohio already knew.

"Her name is Mary. She let me court her in order to get another man's attention. And once she'd done that, she jumped into his wagon, so to speak. Their wedding is coming up." She'd used him, and when he'd realized that, he also understood how all the girls he'd used to feed his ego must have felt. ·

"Oh…that's terrible," she said. "And I agree. You might have had it coming."

Her confirmation stung, but he wasn't going to be derailed now.

"It struck me that I might be fishing with the wrong bait," he said.

"What?" she asked.

"Well…my *daet* used to take me fishing, and he said, if you want trout, don't use catfish bait." Arden leaned forward to check his mirrors and took a firmer hold on the reins as a car passed them. "You're right—I know how to flirt. I know how to get a certain type of girl to like me. But I'm missing something when it comes to finding the kind of woman I need."

"Hmm." She pressed her lips together again. "I don't think you should be using bait at all."

Easy for her to say. She was on the receiving end of the romantic attention.

"That's naive of you," he replied. "You're gorgeous. Men trip over themselves just walking past you. You think that's how things work—you just stand there and men line up. Well, it's not the same for men. We don't just stand there and wait for women to line up for us. We have to go out there and compete for your attention."

"Is that how it works?" She squinted over at him, and he shook his head ruefully.

"*Yah*, Sarai, that's how it works. So I'd better be able to set myself apart from the other men competing for women's attention. That's the challenge."

"I didn't think of that," she murmured.

Had she really never considered what it took for a man to approach a woman? She chided him for being a flirt, but it took guts to put himself out there. Men got rejected again and again. Sometimes, it hurt more than others. Like with Mary—that had hurt deeply.

"So…no advice?" he asked.

She eyed him silently. She wasn't going to help him, was she? And maybe he didn't blame her. He had a lot to make up to her father, and maybe she knew… But before he left Pennsylvania, he was going to pay the man back. He'd have his conscience clear, at least.

"Sarai." Arden smiled over at her hopefully. "Would you be my teacher while I'm here and show me how to attract a good woman? Then I'll leave and never bother you again."

Her cheeks pinkened a little bit, and she looked away. "Stop that."

"Stop what?"

"That smile. That exact smile. Don't you use that on me."

He sighed and dropped the coaxing smile. She'd never fallen for his charms. "Sorry. But will you? This is an old friend asking for your help. I need a quality woman who will work hard with me, be okay with me making less money and be faithful to the family we create. That's what I'm looking for—a woman with character, who will stand by me. And I'll stand by her, too."

"You'll stand by her?" Sarai asked. "Because I won't be partner to you tricking some poor unsuspecting girl in Ohio."

"Of course I will," he said. "I'm looking for marriage now. This is about the rest of my life. I'll be honest and good to her. I promise you that."

Sarai sighed. "Fine."

"That's a *yes*?"

"I will help you learn to attract a good woman." She eyed him warily. "But you'd better drop your flirting ways, Arden Stoltzfus, because it won't do you any good with a woman like that."

"Lesson number one," he said. "And if you catch me flirting by accident, I want you to reach out and smack me."

Sarai burst out laughing and she cast her glittering gaze over him.

"Reach out and smack you?" she laughed. "You have my solemn promise there, Arden." His heart skipped a beat. Sarai was stunningly beautiful—she always had been. And she was smart enough to see straight through him. That was a downright intimidating combination.

Chapter Four

Sarai settled back in the seat as Arden flicked the reins and the horse sped up, the buggy rushing along the pavement. The houses on either side of the road had debris covering their yards, but the damage didn't seem half so bad as at Mammi Ellen's house. One yard had a length of tarp hanging from one tree, and another had a row of bicycles all knocked over in a heap. She leaned forward and waved at a neighbor who was outside with a rake, cleaning up the twigs and leaves that covered her lawn. The older woman waved back.

But the sun shone bright and warm, and the air smelled of sweet summer grass, and if it weren't for the wind damage, she'd never know a storm had passed through their area at all.

"You said Ohio has been difficult. Has your family considered moving back to Pennsylvania?" she asked.

"No. We moved out there for a purpose," he replied.

"I know, I know. You were starting up a new Amish community. I understand that. But it wasn't so hard for your family here, was it?"

"No, not so hard at all," he agreed. "But my *mamm* and *daet* truly believed that Gott wanted us out in Ohio. Mamm said it was like Gott calling Abraham. An adventure."

"You could come back on your own," she said. "I'm sure you could find a job here."

"I could, but it would leave everyone out in our community in Ohio on their own," he said. "Gott called our family. That included me."

"I can appreciate that," she said quietly. She felt that tug toward some change and adventure, too. Was it from Gott? She couldn't say for sure and certain. But it was the kind of tug that wouldn't leave her alone. She was ready for more.

Town was quickly approaching, traffic growing busier along the two-lane road, which broadened to four lanes as they got closer still. A car passed them on the left, and Sarai instinctively leaned back, out of sight. Summer meant more tourists—which was a blessing for the businesses that relied upon the visitors to their area, but it could be trying, too. Traffic was thicker, and a parking spot could be harder to find. At least she wasn't the one with the reins today.

That thought drew her eyes to Arden's strong hands, the leather reins hanging loosely down one palm. His shirtsleeves were rolled up, revealing his tanned, well-muscled forearms. She looked quickly away.

Sarai remembered how her cousin Lizzie used to sigh over how handsome Arden was, and Sarai had simply rolled her eyes.

"Every man has shoulders and arms and eyes and a smile," she'd told her cousin. "Arden is no different."

But he was different, Sarai had to admit. There was something about Arden—some relaxed confidence that made being the woman sitting beside him feel a little safer, whether she wanted to or not. And Sarai did *not* want to feel this.

Arden put his full attention into navigating the roads, and they fell into silence as he drove the buggy into town. He brought them around the back of the hardware store and found one buggy parking spot right under a leafy tree, casting dappled shade for the horse.

"Perfect," Arden said. "The horse will stay cool, at least. I imagine a lot of these people are here for the same reason—that storm was a bad one. I hope they don't sell out of shingles."

He sounded like he was talking to himself more than to her, and Sarai hopped out of the buggy. She glanced toward the street. An Englisher family stood on the opposite sidewalk, all with ice cream cones in their hands as they tried to eat as quickly as possible in the hot sun. A pickup truck passed, and an Englisher young man leaned forward to get a better look at her. She pointedly looked away. She was used to that outsider curiosity, and it was keener from the men her age. They thought she was pretty—she wasn't a complete fool—but she wasn't vain enough to take pleasure in their gawking.

Women had all the same features, too, all wrapped up in different ways. Sure, one might have bluer eyes, and one might be taller, or plumper, or thinner, but it all amounted to the same things. Arms were for hard work and warm hugs. Eyes were for needlework and laughter. The most beautiful part of any woman was her heart, and those Englishers could see nothing of that. Besides, she knew how to deal with them.

Arden waited for her to circle around the buggy before he fell into step beside her, and they headed toward the hardware store together. He walked comfortably close to her, his sleeve brushing hers.

"Do you know the man Mary is going to marry?" she asked, mostly to engage Arden in conversation. If she was busy talking with someone, those Englisher young men were more inclined to leave her alone.

"*Yah*, I know him," Arden said. "His name is Marvin."

"Was he a friend?" she guessed.

"Sort of. Not a lengthy acquaintance or anything, but he was visiting Ohio for a little while, visiting his uncle. I was friendly with him."

"Did you know he was moving in on your girl?" she asked.

"I got the impression," he said dryly. "I figured that if Mary really cared for me, she'd tell him to leave her alone. But she liked him better."

"Ouch." She winced at him. "Maybe you should have said something while you had the chance."

"Maybe..." He shrugged. "I was of the opinion that she should have. Marvin was doing most of this behind my back. At least he and Mary will go settle in Indiana. I won't have to face their happiness at every social gathering."

"Small mercies," she murmured.

They came up the side of the building, and when they emerged onto the sidewalk, she saw a group of four young Englisher men standing by the hardware store. They were drinking cans of Coke—and it did look delicious in this muggy heat—and one of them looked up and his gaze landed on Sarai. She noticed how his gaze softened, and she looked away.

Pretty girls lived their lives trying to avoid unwanted attention. Sometimes she wished Gott had created her just a little bit plainer, less noticeable at first glance. Walking down the street in Redemption on a summer day would be easier that way.

"Hi!" the Englisher called.

Sarai didn't answer, but they'd have to pass the whole group of them to get into the hardware store. She felt Arden tense next to her.

"Just keep walking," Arden murmured in Pennsylvania Dutch, and he touched her back, an indication that he wanted her to hurry along, and she could feel where his thumb had lingered on her spine.

"I said *hi!*" The Englisher was tall, lanky and blond. Not bad-looking—his smile was friendly, not leering. He wore a pair of blue jeans and sandals and a slouchy T-shirt that seemed like it had been mangled by a wringer washer, although the look of being poorly laundered was probably intentional. "I've seen you around before. You normally come with your grandmother, right?"

She shouldn't encourage this, even though the question was innocent enough. So she met his gaze for a moment but didn't answer his question.

"Yeah, I've seen you. I meant to say hello before this, but you run pretty fast." He laughed, his blue eyes sparkling with good humor. "What's your name?"

"Never mind my name," Sarai said.

"Ha!" he said. "So she does speak!"

"Of course I speak," she said, "when I'm with friends. Why should I talk to you?"

The other Englishers laughed. "She's going to school you on your manners, Luke!" one of them said jokingly.

"I'm Luke," he said, rolling his eyes.

"I gathered," she said dryly.

"And you are…?" he prompted with a coaxing smile. "We might count as friends and then we could talk a bit."

She knew exactly what this Luke wanted, and she couldn't very well be keeping company with an Englisher boy. She was well past her *Rumspringa*. He was flirting, and she'd gotten rather good at sidestepping this sort of thing.

"Like I said, never you mind that," she said with a short laugh.

Sarai was about to duck her head and brush past him when the young man put out a hand and touched her arm. It wasn't a threatening move—just an attempt to get her attention—but Arden suddenly slid an arm around her waist. Arden's touch was firm and confident, and she could feel where every single one of his fingers splayed across her side.

"Hey," Arden said, his voice deep and firm, and he tugged Sarai against him. He was warm and solidly muscled. "She's with me."

Sarai's heart sped up, and she felt heat hit her cheeks. She'd never had anyone hold her quite like this before.

"Oh—" The Englisher took a step back. "Sorry, man. No offense."

Arden kept his arm firmly around her waist and only released her when he opened the door and nudged her inside ahead of him.

"Why were you talking to him?" Arden asked as the door shut behind them with a tinkle from the bell overhead. No one had taken notice of their entrance. A clerk was ringing up an older Amish man's order, and she could see some Amish and Englisher customers moving around the store.

"Why?" Sarai asked. "How could I not say something? Was I supposed to pretend I was mute? That was well under control."

"It was not," Arden countered. "You know what he wanted, don't you?"

"I'm very clear on what he wanted!" she retorted. "He wanted my attention. And I wanted to get past. Do you think I never deal with this sort of thing?"

Arden's gaze flashed. "I'm sure you do. But I'm telling you, as a man, that's not the way to do it. You were only encouraging him."

"And you'd know!" Sarai couldn't quite explain the rise of anger. But a few years ago, Arden was just like that Englisher young man—maybe even worse! And he had the gall to lecture her about whether or not she should answer a question?

"*Yah*, I would," Arden retorted, not seeming to quite understand her meaning. "Men take that as encouragement. He got you talking to him. He figured he was ahead of the game."

"There is no game," she shot back.

"There is *always* a game." Arden shook his head. "You know what, Sarai? You are incredibly naive."

An Amish woman that Sarai recognized looked over at them in curiosity, and Sarai felt a rush of embarrassment. Now Arden was going to make her look foolish to boot. So Sarai pulled back her fist and punched him solidly in the shoulder.

It was a shocking thing to do—an Amish woman slugging an Amish man. But he'd asked for it, hadn't he?

"What was that?" Arden looked surprised.

"You said to smack you!" she said.

"I said to smack me if I was flirting." A smile turned up one side of his lips. "I wasn't flirting."

No, he'd been doing something worse.

"You were overstepping. You were pretending to be more to me than you actually are. You were—" He was making her feel warm, protected, and her heart had taken a little tumble. "That wasn't fair. You wanted me to show you how you should behave. Well, that kind of thing is out of bounds. Got it?"

"Okay." He sobered. "Sorry."

"Good." Her gaze slid toward the window, and she saw Luke staring in at her, a curious look on his face. She shook her head and turned away.

"Let's get what we need," she said.

They were here to shop, not argue or make a scene, and Sarai refused to give anyone more reason to talk about them. This had always been the problem with Arden: he never knew when to stop. Maybe what he needed was for a woman he respected to tell him straight when he was messing up. And she was happy to oblige.

Arden looked over his shoulder toward the broad window letting light into the hardware store. This store didn't have electric lights, so it had plenty of windows. The Englisher was peering in them, but when Arden shot him an annoyed look, he turned away. The young men were still hanging around, and he had no doubt that if Sarai left the store without him, Luke would be trying to get her to talk to him again.

Did he blame the guy? Not entirely. Sarai was particularly beautiful, and she didn't seem to know it, either. The Good Book said it best: *like a lily among thorns.* That was what Sarai was like—every other girl paled in comparison to Sarai Peachy. That was just a fact, and he couldn't blame those young men for being hopeful. But Sarai was Amish, and they'd better respect that. That was all he was defending…

Arden headed for the carts, pulled one out with a rattle and started toward the aisle with building supplies. He purposely didn't look in the direction that Sarai went, making his point. He wasn't going to overstep with her. She'd been clear enough.

Maybe Sarai was right: maybe he should have postured a bit more when it came to Mary. But he still thought he shouldn't have to stomp around like a rooster in a henhouse in order to keep a woman faithful to him. The truth was, he'd tried that with Marvin. He'd told him to back off. That didn't work when the woman didn't want defending.

And Sarai didn't want his defending, either.

He used to think he knew his way around the girls. And maybe he had, but he didn't know his boot from his hat when it came to grown women! And he was praying for guidance now. He didn't want to play games. He wanted a woman who'd accept his heart. That was a rarer treasure than he'd ever realized before.

The hardware store carried only one kind of shingle, and he picked up a few packages, mentally tallying up how much he'd need for the stable roof and the chicken coop. Then he grabbed some nails and some tar paper to go underneath it all to protect the roof from the elements. He'd gotten plenty of roofing experience in Ohio—one of the silver linings to having an old house that needed repair.

But he had a different problem here. Dawdie Moe had told him to use the tab. But a tab was simply debt, and somehow he'd gotten the impression that his grandfather wouldn't pay it off easily. Arden had asked a few questions, trying to figure out his grandfather's financial situation, but Dawdie Moe was rather tight-lipped about money.

Sarai had mentioned the egg money at one point. Would she use it for this? Because if he dipped into his savings for repairs, he would be draining away the money he needed to pay her father back.

Sarai came around the corner and spotted him. She had a bag of chicken feed and she dropped it into the cart with a huff of breath.

"There," she said. "Do you have everything?"

"*Yah*, I've got what we need for the roof," he replied.

"Good. Shall we?"

They headed for the register, and Sarai stopped at a bin of cotton yarn.

"I need some for dishcloths," she said, grabbing four skeins and adding them to the cart.

Arden mentally added the price to his tally. Sarai eyed the bin and grabbed two more.

"Sometimes we sell them at the farmers' market, too," she explained.

Right. Of course. He tried to still that wriggle of worry

in his gut as he lifted the items up onto the counter. The cashier was an Amish girl, and she smiled as she started to type the prices into the till.

"Hello," she said. "Arden, you don't remember me, do you?"

He looked up, perplexed. "No, sorry."

"I'm Sadie-Mae," she said.

He racked his brain, then looked up in surprise. "Little Sadie-Mae?"

She'd been one of the kids when he was a teenager—well beneath his age or notice.

"*Yah.* I'm sixteen now," she said.

"Well, hello," he said. "Tell your brother I said hello, too."

"*Yah...*" The girl blushed furiously. "I will."

Sadie-Mae put the items into bags and handed them over. He glanced over at Sarai, and she pulled out some small bills from her purse. Sadie-Mae told them the total, and Sarai passed over sixty dollars in twenties, but the total was far above that. He suppressed a sigh as he pulled out his debit card. He'd have to take care of the rest himself.

"Oh, no," Sarai said, with a quick shake of her head. "Sorry, Arden, I should have been clearer." Then she turned to Sadie-Mae. "Put that on my *daet*'s tab, okay?"

"*Yah*, of course." Sadie-Mae pulled out a book and a nub of pencil and hunched over it, writing carefully.

"Your *daet*'s tab?" That wriggle of worry had started to thrash. "No, that's not right. I'll take care of it."

"It's for my grandmother's home," Sarai said. "You don't need to pay for that. This is how we do things."

Sadie-Mae looked up, hesitant. "Go on and put it on his tab."

Sadie-Mae passed the notebook over for Sarai to see. No wonder Sarai was so free and easy with adding to the cart—her egg money didn't cover half of their needs. Her *daet* paid for the rest. He shouldn't be surprised, of course, and it was a relief that the financial burden wouldn't be his for this particular shopping trip, but it did explain a lot.

"*Yah*, that looks right," Sarai said. "*Danke*, Sadie-Mae."

"You're welcome. See you Sunday for service."

"See you."

Sarai turned to give him a smile. "Sorry about that, Arden. I can't imagine what you were thinking with me filling up the cart like that. I wouldn't do that to you!"

He smiled faintly. "It would have been fine. It's okay."

He couldn't exactly admit that it would have been a hardship, could he? But Sarai was obviously a young woman who was used to a comfortable life. She bought what she needed and didn't seem to even consider the total at the end of the trip. But then, her *daet*'s farm was large by Amish standards, and they were very comfortable.

"Well, Mammi Ellen would have schooled me for an hour if I'd done that to you," Sarai said. "I saved myself a lecture."

"'Bye, Arden," Sadie-Mae said, then after a beat, "and 'bye, Sarai."

"'Bye." Arden shot the girl a smile, and her blush only deepened. It made him chuckle as he turned away, but then he looked at Sarai hesitantly.

"Do I get smacked for that?" he asked.

"No, that couldn't be helped," Sarai said, looking over her shoulder. "But Sadie-Mae might need a word of wisdom or two."

To warn her about men like him? That stung. Arden regretted his choices back then, but he hardly thought he was bad enough to warrant that. Maybe he had been. Maybe he'd caused more damage than he'd realized...

They headed for the door, Arden carrying two heavy bags in one hand, a roll of tar paper under his arm and a bag of chicken feed under the other arm. Sarai carried a single bag with her knitting cotton. He could see the Englisher young men still outside, their laughter and chatting voices just loud enough to be heard.

Sarai had made it clear that she didn't want his interference, and this time he wasn't going to say a thing. But he could see an uncertain look on her face as they approached the door, and as they stepped outside, she took the roll of tar paper out from under his arm—it was heavy, but she managed it—and slipped her hand around his bicep. It felt nice.

The Englishers stopped talking as they came out, but they didn't say anything, and Arden and Sarai carried on past them and headed toward the side of the building to go to the back parking lot. When they'd turned the corner, she released his arm.

"What was that?" he asked with a small smile.

"What?" But there was color in her cheeks.

"You held my arm," he said. "I daresay you pretended that you *were* with me."

"It was easier than dealing with them nagging me," she replied. "Maybe you had a point about that."

"And you don't think taking my arm like that was maybe sending *me* the wrong message?" He was teasing her now, but he couldn't help it. She'd made him feel about as foolish as a five-year-old back there. "What if I got the impression that you wanted me to court you?"

"I hardly think—"

"I might need to warn the young men about *you*," he countered jokingly.

She swatted his arm, and he laughed.

"A woman as pretty as you had better be careful," he said. "A man is apt to get the wrong impression and think he has a chance."

"Well, you don't," she said, but there was laughter in her eyes now. "And don't you forget it."

But he had liked the way it felt when she took his arm that way. He'd felt strong, capable…like he was her protector. And if that Englisher—Luke, was it?—had started up again, he would have postured a bit to make sure the message was abundantly clear. He hadn't been joking about the effect she had on men…on him. She made him want to be a bit bigger, a bit stronger and worthy of her trust when she walked through a crowd of interested Englishers.

Sarai hoisted herself up into the buggy, and Arden went around to put the supplies into the back. Then he pulled himself up and settled next to her. The horse took a couple of steps backward, eager to get moving again.

"Can I ask you something?" he said as the horse pulled them through the parking lot toward the road.

"Sure," she replied.

"Does your *daet* pay for everything for your *mammi*?" he asked.

"Not everything," she replied. "She has some money of her own, but when we need to, we put things on his tab. He doesn't mind."

"Hmm."

"Why?" she asked.

"Nothing. Just wondering," he replied.

"Should he not take care of his own *mamm*?" Sarai asked.

"Of course he should!" he replied. "It's not that. I was just wondering if maybe we should have been doing something like that for my *dawdie*."

"Oh…" She was silent for a moment. "I don't know. He eats with us fairly often, so he isn't suffering, I can assure you."

"I didn't think he was," he said. "But we've got to think ahead, that's all. I mean, if he won't come back with me."

The problem was his family could never afford to simply have a tab running for Dawdie that they paid off every month. There were doctor appointments and his mother's root canal and various other fixes that needed done around the farm. The bit of extra money Arden had been able to save up on his own, he'd tucked away for a wedding. When Mary dumped him, he knew what he needed to do with that money. He needed to make things square with Job Peachy.

When he was a teen, he'd damaged Job's brand-new buggy. Job had no idea it was Arden, but that didn't make a difference. Arden had wanted sincere regret and confession to Gott to be enough, but it wasn't. Making this truly right would also include making restitution. He'd have to pay Job the full amount for the buggy he'd totaled that fateful night. Although, Arden didn't even have enough money set aside for that. He'd simply have to give Job the money he had and promise him more as he was able to set it aside.

Restitution was the hard part. And Arden couldn't avoid doing the right thing any longer.

But when he glanced over at Sarai, another thought was simmering in his mind, too. He was thinking that, pretty as she was, and as much as she made him want to grow three inches of height just to better protect her, she was used to a certain level of comfort that he'd never be able to provide. If Gott hadn't blessed him with enough money to make his own sins right, then Redemption was going to have to remain firmly in his past.

So whatever protective, softer feelings were starting to stir inside of him, he'd better tamp them down now. He owed her father too much as it was. Sarai Peachy was worried about him leading on susceptible women, but his heart was far more vulnerable than she gave him credit for.

And so was his lashed conscience.

Chapter Five

When they got back to the house, the sun was still high in the sky. The day was hot, and it felt good to step out of the buggy and let a breeze cool Sarai's back in the shade beside the buggy shed on Dawdie Moe's farm. A cow and her large calf were by the fence, and they mooed at Sarai. She looked at them for a moment, then turned back toward Arden. He had started to unhitch the horse.

"What did you mean when you said that there's always a game going on?" she asked.

Arden chuckled, then headed around the back of the buggy and grabbed the bags. When he reemerged, he said, "It's ironic that I'd be the one to break this to you, Sarai, but you are uncommonly beautiful. That's why the men pester you." He carried the bags, one in each hand, and he jutted his chin toward Mammi's property next door. "Let's get moving."

Uncommonly beautiful. No one had ever used those words to her before. Her mother had told her that she was "sensibly put together by Gott Himself" and shouldn't get her head all puffed up about length of limb or brightness of eye.

Sarai fell into step beside Arden. He wasn't flirting now, and he certainly wasn't one of the men trying to get her to smile, so she felt more comfortable with him.

"My *mamm* always said that any woman is beautiful to a hungry man so long as she's got a platter of fried chicken in her hands," Sarai said as they walked through the short grass, grasshoppers jumping up out of the scrub like little bullets, shooting out of the way.

Arden barked out a laugh. "*Yah,* I suppose she's right. But some girls don't require the chicken. That's all I'm saying."

Sarai rolled her eyes. "Eventually, given enough time, he's going to want the chicken."

"Probably."

Sarai laughed. "At last, we agree."

But his compliment still sat warm in her heart. He thought she was uncommonly beautiful—and he said it without any attempt to win her over. Perhaps he'd be able to give her some honest advice about men, too. Perhaps they both could learn something that would benefit them later.

When Sarai and Arden walked up to the house, she spotted her grandmother, bending over in the garden, picking cucumbers, dropping them with a soft thunk into the plastic bucket that Moe held out for her. Most of the garbage had been cleaned up from around the yard, and a pile waited beside the drive.

Sarai paused and watched the older people while Arden carried the bags of supplies over to the stable. Mammi dropped another cucumber into the bucket, and then both old people leaned over the top of it, peering inside.

Sarai couldn't hear what they were saying from here, but then they turned and saw Sarai. Mammi Ellen smiled and waved, and she and Moe came out of the garden rows, stepping carefully over the leafy cucumber plants. As Mammi came to the last row to step over, Moe held a hand out, and she took his fingers as she made the last hop.

Yah…only old friends…of course! But Sarai could see a spark of something significantly more than that. An old friend wouldn't be offering Mammi his hand or looking at her with such tenderness in his eyes.

Sarai looked over to where Arden stood, his gaze fixed on the roof.

"We need a ladder, Arden," Sarai said.

"*Yah*. Do you have one?"

"It's inside. I'll get it."

Sarai followed Mammi Ellen and Moe into the house, the screen door clapping shut behind her. The older folks moved into the kitchen, and Mammi brought the cucumbers to the sink and turned on the water.

"We'll have cucumber salad with dinner tonight," Mammi said.

"I do enjoy a good cucumber salad," Moe said appreciatively. "I can help with the peeling, Ellen."

"Oh, I know, Moe," Ellen said as Sarai went down the cellar stairs. She could hear their voices filtering down to her. "You have the touch when it comes to peeling…"

The ladder was leaning against one wall, and she grabbed it. It was tall, but too unwieldly for her to carry by herself. She banged it against a couple of steps on her way up, and then the door opened. She expected to see Moe at the top of the stairs, but it was Arden instead.

"You can't carry that alone," Arden said.

"I'm fine," she replied.

Arden shook his head, came down the staircase to meet her and took one end of the ladder. It was easier work carrying it with his help, and they came up into the kitchen, then toward the door once more.

"Have you thought of eating a sandwich, Ellen?" Moe asked, catching Sarai's eye.

"What's that?" Mammi said. "I don't want to ruin my appetite."

"But you need energy, too," Moe countered. "Maybe just a piece of bread and butter."

"Are you saying that *you* want a sandwich, Moe?"

"No, I'm saying—"

Sarai and Arden emerged outside, and Sarai couldn't help but laugh.

"Your *dawdie* is doing a good job taking care of Mammi Ellen," she said.

"Yah." Arden frowned, looking toward the house again.

"You can't tell me you didn't see that between them, Arden," Sarai said, lowering her voice.

They carried the ladder between them over to the stable, and then Arden set it up.

"They're friends," he said.

"They care for each other," Sarai said. "If you didn't know them, you would have thought they were an old married couple."

"If people didn't know us in town, they might think the same thing," he said.

"That's not fair," she said. "I held your arm to keep those Englishers from bothering me."

"And Dawdie is just trying to keep your grandmother from overexerting herself," he replied, picking up both bags in one hand and then putting a hand on the ladder. He sighed and looked over at Sarai. "Here's the thing, Sarai. Maybe they feel some tenderness between them, and maybe they're just old friends. But the fact of the matter remains that we, his family, can't afford to send money."

"You can't?" The words were out before she could rethink them.

"No, we can't." She noticed the color in his face. "Ohio hasn't been as easy to settle in as we'd hoped. It's been a hard start, and we've had a few setbacks, as you've heard. But it's worse than that. My family needs my income to make ends meet, and if we're going to take care of Dawdie, we have to bring him into our home. There is no extra money to just send him something when he needs it."

"I thought you said earlier that you were thinking about doing just that," she countered.

His ears turned red. "I was embarrassed, Sarai! I didn't want to admit it."

"Oh… I'm sorry."

"It's fine. It's better to have it out and stop making things worse with my own pride." He pulled off his hat and ran a hand through his hair. "And I refuse to have my *dawdie* resting on the charity of this community when he's got a family to take care of him. Or resting on your father's generosity. What kind of man would I be if I was okay with that?"

They couldn't afford it… She hadn't realized it was that bad. Then she remembered her worries about the Stoltzfus motivation to get Moe off that farm. Was it only to care for an old man, or were there members of that family who wanted more from Moe, like the farm?

"What will happen to his farm when he leaves?" she asked.

"It's going to my uncle when Dawdie passes, but until then, I suppose someone will rent it," he replied. "My uncle will deal with that, since he'll be inheriting."

"Why doesn't your uncle help Dawdie now?" she asked.

"Because everyone is in agreement that Dawdie needs to come be with family," Arden replied. "This is out of my hands, Sarai. Do you think I have any authority at all in this decision?"

She knew he didn't have any more authority than she did. They were not the generation who held the reins here, but there was more to this than Arden was telling her. She could feel it.

"Will your uncle sell it?" Sarai asked.

"I don't know." Arden just shrugged. "Maybe. Again, that's out of my hands. Look, I know you want our grandparents together, Sarai, but this isn't a decision based on romantic notions. This is a realistic conclusion. There isn't enough money to keep him here on his own land if he needs any extra help to stay here. We just don't have it."

She understood now. This was why he had to bring his grandfather back. But Sarai wasn't a woman who gave up so easily. If Mammi and Moe had feelings for each other, there had to be a solution that allowed them to be together—even if it trampled some Stoltzfus pride.

Arden climbed up the ladder carefully, carrying his load of supplies in one hand as he ascended. He disliked having to break it down like that for Sarai. He'd seen the surprise in her face as she realized what he meant: they were poor.

It hit like a punch to the gut. He hated that.

Some days, Arden was frustrated with his parents for that move to Ohio. It hadn't been a good one for the family finances, but it had been an adventure, for sure and certain. And it had given him his longed-for fresh start. That move had pulled them all—his family and the other three families who had moved out there—a little closer together as they worked to start a life as a fledgling Amish community.

Sometimes the things Gott asks us to do aren't easy, his father said again and again. *Just because it's hard doesn't mean it isn't going to be beautiful when we're done.*

But on days like this one when he was forced to explain in excruciating detail just how tight their finances were, it was hard to keep the more positive perspective. He put the bags of supplies down on the sloped, shingled roof.

Gott, please give me the money to make things right with Job. I feel Your nudge to fix this, but You haven't given me enough to offer him restitution. If You'd just bless us for a little while, maybe I could!

He'd prayed this same prayer every time his conscience had pricked him over the last four years, and Gott hadn't answered him yet. It wasn't that Arden didn't want to make things right.

He looked down and saw Sarai, her hands on her hips, her chin tipped up. He nodded toward the tools he'd forgotten on the ground. "Can you bring those hammers up to me?"

"Sure."

Sarai picked them up and started up the ladder. She appeared over the edge of the roof, and as she came up, the tools in one hand, he reached out to catch her free hand to give her some balance as she came up the last rung onto the sloped roof. He gave her a gentle tug to keep her moving in the right direction, but his tug was a little too strong, because he pulled her right up to him, her dress brushing against his pants. She looked as surprised as he felt, her blue eyes wide. He could see a stray eyelash on her cheek, and the spattering of faint freckles covering her nose, and his breath caught.

"Oh…" she whispered, then held up the hammers. "For you."

"Thank you." He swallowed. There was a time a few years ago when he might have taken advantage of a moment like this one, but not anymore. He took a careful step back.

"You know, if I were you, I'd just move back to Redemption."

"I have some things holding me back," he said.

"Like what?"

He squatted down and started to pry up nails and damaged shingles. "Like the fact that I like myself better in Ohio."

He didn't have quite so many regrets out there, not so many reminders of things he'd messed up.

"Why do you like yourself better in Ohio than here? You're the same man."

"No, I'm not," he replied.

She eyed him but didn't say anything. Arden pried up two more nails and tossed a split shingle to the side.

"Look, in Ohio, I'm the middle son of a new farmer in the area. I'm just Arden—someone people don't know very well yet. They know I work hard, and if you've got a broken fence, I'm the one to ask because I can fix a fence faster than your cows can get out. They know I'm looking to get married, and they know that I was courting Mary and she left me for Marvin. These are all families coming from different communities. We've known each other for four years. We don't have any other history."

"Sounds lonely," she said.

"It's not."

"Your history is who you are."

He rocked back on his heels and looked up at her. "No, it isn't."

"Of course it is! My history tells people what I stand for and who I come from. If you know my history, you know me."

For her, maybe. He could understand what she meant, but it was different for him.

"My history here in Redemption doesn't tell anyone the truth of what's inside of me," he replied. "It shows who I used to be, not who I am now."

"And who are you now?" she asked.

"I'm Arden Stoltzfus, middle son of an Amish farmer,"

he repeated. "I'm a hard worker and a solid friend. I'm a Christian, and I try to do what's right."

She was silent again, but this time he shut his mouth. She'd asked, and that was his answer.

"That's it?" she said after a couple of beats.

"That's it."

"Well, I think you're more than that," she said.

His breath caught, and he tried to shove away a little surge of hope that she'd say she saw more in his character.

"You're your history, too," she concluded.

And that whisper of hope evaporated. Right. Of course. And this was exactly why he was currently so glad to face the tough life in Ohio. Everyone here in Redemption knew all his mistakes, his ungraceful moments, his embarrassments… People here knew too much.

"So are you going to help me or what?" he said.

Sarai went down to her hands and knees, and she started working on the shingle next to him, prying up the first nail.

"You say my history is a big part of who I am, but you judge me for my history," Arden said.

"Maybe I do…a little bit," Sarai said. "But it doesn't make it any less a part of you. You're just running away from who you are, Arden."

She pulled up the second nail with a squeak, and Arden tossed it into the pile for her.

"Oh, I'm definitely running away," Arden replied. "But I'm running from who I *was*. Ohio is a fresh start for me, and maybe no one really deserves a clean slate, but I'm going to take it all the same."

A buggy turned into the drive, the clop of the horse's hooves floating across the summer breeze toward them. Arden pulled off his hat and wiped his forehead. He recognized the farmer with the reins in his hands. It was Job Peachy.

"My father's here," Sarai said.

Arden watched as the buggy rattled up the drive. Job was a big man, and his beard was bushy and streaked with gray. Sarai stood up and brushed off her hands. Arden grabbed another loose shingle and pulled it off the last nail that held it in place. He had a job to do.

"I'd better go down there and talk to him," Sarai said.

"Of course," he replied. "I'll take care of the roof. It's no problem."

"I said I'd help you," she said. "I'll be back."

"Don't worry about it," he replied. "You'll be busy with your family."

Besides, when this roofing patch was done, the effectiveness of the work was going to speak for him long after he was gone. It would be nice to have one thing in Redemption that spoke well of him.

Sarai went back down the ladder, and he watched as she jogged across the grass toward her father's buggy. He reined in the horse and hopped down. Their voices didn't carry, but Job hugged his daughter and then looked around the yard. Then his gaze moved up to the stable roof. The older man gave Arden a hard stare, and Arden raised one hand in a wave.

Should he go down and say hello? It was the polite thing to do, and he was working on Job's mother's stable roof. He had intended to visit Job before he left, but

Arden wasn't ready for that conversation yet. It was one he'd have to work up the courage for and then be able to think it over while he was traveling back to Ohio.

Job headed over in his direction and stopped a few yards away. The older man shaded his eyes past the brim of his straw hat to look up at him. Sarai followed her father, and when they stood side by side, Arden could see the family resemblance between the two in their blue eyes and the way they stood.

"Hello, Arden," Job said.

"Hello," Arden said. "The shingles came off the roof here, and I'm fixing it."

"Danke," Job said. "It's kind of you to do that."

"It's not a problem. I'm just here for a week or so with my grandfather."

"How's he holding up?" Job asked.

"Good." Arden nodded.

"He and my mother are good friends," Job said. "If I can help your *dawdie* out in any way, let me know."

"Danke," Arden said. He'd noticed that Job was talking to him like a man now, and he liked that feeling. Perhaps things had changed around here a little bit, too.

"And your parents?" Job asked. "How is Ohio doing for your family?"

"We're in Gott's hands," Arden said.

Job smiled and nodded. "Amen. A *gut* place to be. Well, I'd best check in with my mother and see what she needs. That was some storm. Thank you again for your help with that roof. I hope the supplies didn't cost you anything."

"No, Daet, I wouldn't do that. We covered some of

it with the egg money, and I put the rest on your tab," Sarai said.

There was a pause, and Job shot his daughter a thoughtful look. "Good. Good. Well… I'll just head inside."

Job turned toward the house, and Arden felt a surge of frustration. They'd put the rest of the supplies for Job's mother's repairs on Job's tab, and Arden couldn't help but feel he'd missed an opportunity to prove himself a better man. Ironically, it would only come out of the money Arden would be handing over to Job anyway. Still…he never seemed to get it right in Redemption, somehow.

"I think I made a mistake there," Arden said.

Sarai moved closer to the stable and looked up at him. "I don't think so. Why?"

But that had been a subtle communication between men, and she seemed not to have noticed. He couldn't blame her—he was lost on most of the subtleties when women talked to each other, too. But her father had expected something a little more from him, and he hadn't delivered.

"Never mind," Arden said. "I'd better get this done."

Sarai eyed him for a moment thoughtfully—a whole lot like her father had—then turned back toward the house. He watched her pink cape dress swish as she walked, and she looked so fresh and bright out there in the summer sunlight.

Then he picked up the hammer and turned back to prying out the old nails. Job would know the worst before Arden headed back home again, so if he was sensing that Arden wasn't measuring up, then he was right.

Gott had given Arden a second chance in Ohio, and once he could convince his grandfather to go back with him, he wasn't going to squander it.

Chapter Six

Sarai headed into the house behind her father, and before the screen door bounced shut, she looked back again toward the stable. Arden crouched on the roof, and she could see him pull up a nail and then lean forward again. How much was Arden hiding? It wasn't like she'd ever known him very well. She'd been aware of the swath of heartbreak he left behind him. He looked up from his work and gazed in her direction.

Sarai's heartbeat sped up, and she wondered if her suspicion showed on her face. She turned into the house and followed her father into the kitchen.

"It looks like your place took a walloping, Mamm," Job said. "Our farm got a bit of a wind, but nothing like out here."

"*Yah*, it blew pretty hard," Mammi replied. "The chicken coop roof went flying clear across the backyard."

Moe pushed himself to his feet, and he gave Job a friendly smile and nod.

"Good to see you, Job."

"You, too, Moe."

"I'd best get back to my own place. I have chores waiting," Moe said, and he headed toward the door, then looked past Sarai and Job. "I'll see you later on, Ellen!"

"*Yah*, come for dinner tonight," Mammi replied. "I'm planning chili—the way you like it. I figure you and Arden will have worked up a mighty appetite, and I want to pay you back for all this work."

"There is no payment needed," Moe said. "You know that, Ellen. But I'll gratefully eat your cooking."

Moe shot Sarai and Job a smile. "I'll leave you to your family visit, then."

The old man headed out the door without another word.

"Did you hear the storm last night?" Job asked once Moe's boots had thumped down the steps outside.

"Sarai slept through the whole thing," Mammi said. "I heard it blowing, but I put it into Gott's hands, rolled over and went back to sleep. Staring out a window at a storm I can't control doesn't help anyone, now, does it?"

"No, Mamm, you're right there," Job agreed. "Well, I'll pull some people together to help you out with that coop."

"Moe and Arden are already offering," Mammi said.

"Well, a few more wouldn't hurt," Job replied. "Where are you putting the chickens in the meantime?"

"That'll take some work," Sarai said, speaking up for the first time. "I'll have to set up a new enclosure with chicken wire to keep the birds all together."

Her father shot her a smile. "I'll pass the word. To-morrow, we'll have it all fixed up. Instead of a barn rais-ing, we'll have a coop raising."

Sarai laughed at his little joke. "Thank you, Daet."

"Now, regarding Moe..." Job sobered. "Mamm, the bishop received a letter from Moe's son Ezekiel in Ohio."

"Wanting him to move back," Mammi Ellen said with a nod.

Sarai's father was a local deacon, and he was often privy to the internal workings of the community.

"Did Moe mention it to you?" Job asked.

"No, but Sarai told me," Mammi said with a sad nod.

"Arden told me," Sarai offered quietly.

"Ah. And? Does he want to go?" her father asked.

"I haven't brought it up with him yet," Mammi said. "I suppose I'm afraid he'll want to leave, and I'm not ready to hear it."

"It did occur to me that someone might try to pressure him to do something he doesn't want to do," Sarai said.

"Someone?" Her father smoothed his beard. "Like Arden, you mean?"

"Arden has no more authority in this than I do," Sarai said. "But someone in the family might have reason to get their hands on Moe's farm. It would be terrible to have Moe pushed off his own land before he's ready to go. That's all I'm saying."

"Well, the bishop and the elders and the rest of the deacons all agree that the Stoltzfus family is doing the right thing to take care of him the best way they know how," Job said.

"He's not that old," Mammi said.

"Well, he's old enough," Job countered.

"Are you calling me old?" she sniffed.

"I wouldn't dream of it, Mamm," Job replied. "But you have Sarai living with you, me a twenty-minute ride from you and a whole lot more support than Moe's got."

"Moe has Mammi," Sarai said softly. "And me. And you."

"Moe's not *ours*," Job said gently. "I'm fond of old Moe, too, Sarai, but he's got a family who need him around. He's got grandchildren who deserve time with him while they have him."

"Oh, Daet, you sound like he's some doddering old man. He's not! He's got lots of energy, and he's witty and funny and keeps his farm running. In fact, I think he could even get married again. He's a nice-looking man still, and he's got the kindest eyes, don't you think, Mammi?"

Job slowly turned toward Sarai and fixed her with a mildly surprised look. "Excuse me?"

Why was everyone so against Moe still living his life? It looked like she had a few more seeds to plant in that respect.

"What's so shocking about that?" Sarai asked. "He's got lots of life left in him."

"She's not thinking of marrying him herself," Mammi said with a low laugh.

Job heaved a sigh and scrubbed a hand through his gray-tinged hair. "Well, that's a relief!"

"Not me, Daet!" Sarai said and laughed. "All I'm saying is everyone is acting like Moe has one foot in the grave, and he doesn't."

"Would you do that to me?" Mammi asked Job seriously. "Would you decide my time in my own house was up and cart me off to one of your homes, whether I was ready to say goodbye to my old house or not?"

"Mamm…" Job said.

"Well, would you?" Mammi asked. "Because that's

what's happening here. No one is asking Moe what's good for him. Everyone is just deciding for him. I'll have you know, son, that Sarai has a good point. Just because we get old and our bodies age doesn't mean our minds melt away. Some days, in my heart I'm still a young mother with a baby in my arms. Other days, I feel like that woman in her forties who has such a busy home. Other days, I feel fifty again or sixty... I might have gotten old, but I'm still your mother, Job."

"Mamm, how did this become about you?" Job asked softly. "I'm not sending you anywhere, okay? You'll stay in your house as long as you want to."

Mammi Ellen nodded. "And while you are remembering that you'd never do such a thing to your own mother, I'd like you to remember that Moe deserves the same treatment that I do."

Job sighed. "Of course, Mamm. But this isn't about wanting him to go or wanting him to stay. This is about a family working together for their elder. They're doing their best, and they need our support."

Sarai's father didn't stay too much longer. He had the cows to milk and other work waiting for him, so he headed out again with repeated promises that they'd sort out the coop the next day. For one night, the roof would just have to be set back on top of the frame and tacked down with a few nails. It would do.

When Sarai and Mammi were alone in the kitchen again, Sarai cast her grandmother a smile.

"You stood up for yourself very well, Mammi," she said.

"I'm your father's mother," Mammi replied. "There is a certain understanding between mothers and sons."

"Does he know what Moe means to you?" Sarai asked.

Mammi sobered, and she sighed. "No. I don't believe he does."

"It might be worth telling him," Sarai said.

"Sarai, your *daet* is right. That family is only trying to take care of Moe. That's a time that comes for all of us. But it doesn't mean it's any easier on us old folks." Mammi headed toward the counter. "Let's get dinner started. Moe and Arden will be hungry."

It was as close to an admission of tender feelings that Sarai could get out of her grandmother right now, but she'd seen how passionately Mammi had argued for Moe, and Sarai couldn't help but smile to herself as she tied on her work apron and went to wash her hands.

Dinner that night would consist of Mammi's meaty chili, a noodle casserole and some skillet corn bread. Mammi was particular about her chili, and so she started the pot on the back of the stove with all of her ingredients to simmer. Sarai chopped onions, celery and zucchini from the garden, and she could hear Arden pounding nails now—*thwack, thwack*. Never more than two blows with the hammer.

Would Arden really work against Mammi and Moe getting together? It sounded like everyone was against it, and Arden was here on a mission to bring his grandfather home. She now understood a little bit better about their financial constraints, but was there really no other solution?

The hammering stopped, and Sarai went over to the window to look outside. Arden was opening a new package of shingles, from what Sarai could tell.

"The two of you seem to be getting along," Mammi said.

"I suppose." She went back to her chopping. "You know the kind of flirt Arden always was, so if you're suggesting more than two people getting along…"

"*Yah*, he sure was a flirt," Mammi agreed. "I was afraid back then that Lizzie would marry him."

There wasn't any risk of that. No girl had been able to rope Arden. For a couple of minutes they worked in silence, and Sarai swept the vegetables off her cutting board and into a big mixing bowl. But her mind kept going back to that conversation on the stable roof.

"Let me ask you this, Mammi," Sarai said. "If I am one way here in Redemption, and I go to visit Katie in Shipshewana, would I be a different person out there?"

Mammi paused in her stirring, then shrugged. "No, I don't think so. Are you thinking of going for a visit to see your cousin, dear?"

"That's not what I mean, exactly," she hedged, because she couldn't go to Shipshewana for her own fresh start with things the way they stood, anyway. Mammi needed someone with her. "What I mean is, hypothetically speaking, if I went to Shipshewana, everything that mattered—my character, my faith, my beliefs—they would all be the same, right?"

"*Yah*," Mammi said. "I should certainly hope so!"

"Well, Arden likes who he is better in Ohio. That's what he says, at least. And I don't think a person changes all that much just by putting him in a different state. It doesn't change our weaknesses or our strengths or… anything! It's just a change of scenery. No place has that power over us."

"I daresay you're right," Mammi said. "But isn't that

the lure of a fresh start? You can be anyone you want to be if you start out right."

When Sarai didn't answer, Mammi nodded toward the big black skillet hanging on a hook on the wall. "I need you to start the corn bread. Do you mind?"

"Of course I'll do it," Sarai replied.

And she pulled the skillet off the hook and brought it to the hot woodstove. She pried the cover off the burner with a hook, put the skillet on top of the open circle and placed a lump of lard in the bottom of the pan. It took a moment, and then it started to melt.

But while Arden's insistence that his past wasn't a part of him annoyed her, a different small worry had started to form in the back of Sarai's mind. When people moved away, they oftentimes didn't move back. Arden certainly wasn't going to. She was just now realizing that if she went to Shipshewana and met a farmer to marry, she might never live in Redemption again, and that thought brought a lump to her throat.

Arden might be perfectly happy to leave this place behind like some old disappointment, but she was not. Redemption had formed the best parts of her.

Early that evening, Arden walked next to his grandfather back toward the Peachy property. The sun had sunk lower in the sky, but it still shone hot. Arden had finished the roof on the Peachy stable. There would be no leaking from the area he'd patched up—that much was sure. And after he and Dawdie had washed their faces and hands and changed their clothes, they headed over to the neighbors' house for dinner.

"Ellen sure can cook," Dawdie Moe said. "You're in for a treat. You know, if you stayed around here…"

"Dawdie, I can't stay," Arden said.

"But if you did, you'd be able to eat rather well visiting Ellen Peachy from time to time, I can tell you that."

Arden just smiled. It was hard to argue with that. Dawdie was probably right, but Arden wasn't staying. Here in Redemption, he felt like his old reputation haunted him. He'd have to stand shoulder to shoulder with the fathers of the girls he'd flirted with, and he'd have to face Job Peachy, too. His future was not in Redemption.

"Have you never even considered it?" Dawdie asked. "I could sure use some help around the farm."

"You're supposed to come home with me." That was the solution. That was their duty as his family.

"But what if you stayed here instead?" Dawdie asked.

What if…? The farm didn't make much. It was small, and a lot of the equipment needed replacing. Would he make enough to pay back what he owed to Job? Not likely. Besides, as he'd told Sarai, he liked himself better in Ohio. He was a better version of himself there. In Ohio, he was helping to build something from the floorboards on up. In Pennsylvania, he was trying to repair something he'd already broken.

"Dawdie, I'm helping my parents," he said. "They need me, too."

It was part of his reason, at least.

"Of course, of course…" But he heard the disappointment in the old man's voice.

Arden found himself looking forward to seeing Sarai again tonight. He'd told himself he wouldn't do this, though. He was ready to put Redemption behind him and bring his grandfather home.

Dawdie walked with a more confident stride as they headed across the grass, and his hat was set at a slightly jaunty angle. The house was within sight, and Arden noticed a smudge of smoke coming out a window. His heart skipped a beat, but then the door opened and a puff of smoke came out and melted way into the air. As it cleared, Sarai appeared with a kitchen towel and flapped it back and forth. She froze when she spotted them, and Arden smiled ruefully and waved.

"Hello!" Sarai called. She started flapping the towel again.

"A kitchen mishap," Dawdie said. "Let's walk a little slower, Arden."

"Are you sure?" he asked.

"*Yah*, I'm sure. Let the smoke clear," he said. "And then we will very politely eat whatever is placed in front of us."

"I know how to be polite," Arden said with a laugh.

"Good." Dawdie shot him a sidelong look. "Then we should have no problems."

He'd been in Ohio, not in a hole somewhere, but he could appreciate his grandfather's desire to protect the women's feelings. They slowed their pace, and Sarai flapped her towel a little bit more, then headed back into the house.

When they arrived, the house still smelled of burned cooking, and Ellen let them in with a bright smile. A lingering film of smoke filled the mudroom.

"You men have been working so hard today," she said. "We can't thank you enough for all your help."

"We're happy to do it, Ellen," Dawdie Moe said with a smile.

"Very happy," Arden said.

He let the older people move into the kitchen first, and when he stepped out of the mudroom, he spotted Sarai standing by the stove, her cheeks red.

"I'm sorry to have burned half the dinner," Sarai said. "We wanted to serve corn bread with the chili, but—" She gestured vaguely to the skillet behind her. It was nicely browned on top, but it was smoking from the bottom of the pan, from what Arden could make out.

"It looks fine to me," Moe said.

"Oh, Moe," Sarai chuckled. "You'd be wrong, just this once."

"It's just a little browned," Moe said. "I'll take a piece to go with my chili, if you don't mind." His grandfather poked him in the ribs with an elbow.

"So will I," Arden said quickly.

"You will?" Sarai turned her attention to Arden then, and she gave him a wry smile. "You don't have to do this, Arden."

"I think I do," he said, eyeing his grandfather. "Besides, when my *mamm* is working some evenings at the farmers' market, I'm the one who makes dinner. And I can assure you, your cooking is a step up from my own."

Sarai took a knife and began to cut the corn bread in the skillet. It would be badly burned on the bottom, but he'd committed to eating it now. His grandfather knew a thing or two about pleasing women, it would seem. Maybe he could take a few tips from the old man, as well. Although, he had a feeling that if he'd been the one to suggest that the meal was perfectly edible as it was, Sarai wouldn't have taken it the same way.

"Come sit down," Ellen said, gesturing to the table, already set with plates and cutlery.

Arden took a chair next to his grandfather, and Ellen seated herself across the table from Moe. When Sarai joined them, they all bowed their heads for a moment of silent grace, and then when Moe cleared his throat, the prayer was over.

"Sarai, you make a very good corn bread," Moe said, accepting a scorched piece from her.

"I'm not sure I deserve the compliment this time, Moe," she said.

"A little browning doesn't change facts, my dear girl," Moe replied. Then he accepted a bowl of chili from Ellen. "And, Ellen, I don't think I've ever tasted better chili than yours."

Dawdie Moe was quite the sweet-talker. Maybe Arden could see why Sarai thought Moe and Ellen would be such a good match, if his grandfather acted like this...

"Moe, you are a very good man," Sarai said earnestly. "I mean it. And I know that my family thinks very well of you."

"Well..." Moe's cheeks pinkened. *"Danke."*

"I mean it, Moe," she said. "I really do wish you'd think about having a wife again, because you have so much to offer a home. You really do."

Ellen reached over under the table, and Arden couldn't see what she did, but Sarai gave a little jump.

"Moe, have you ever seen such weather?" Ellen asked sweetly, cutting her granddaughter a flat look, and Arden smothered a smile. It seemed that Ellen wasn't blind to what Sarai was up to, and that was good to see.

The older people settled into a conversation about windstorms they'd seen over the years, and Arden looked across the table at Sarai.

"You aren't very subtle," he said quietly.

Sarai looked toward the older people and lowered her voice. "I can't be. I don't have much time, do I?"

"Are you telling me you had a long game for this, and it was more discreet?" Arden teased softly. He looked up to make sure the older folks couldn't hear them, and they were engrossed in their own conversation.

"Yes, I did. It would have taken six months, I believe, and at the end of it, I would have shown these two what they needed to see." She kept her voice low, too, but she wasn't joking, though. So there *was* a long game here… He shook his head.

"Sarai, I told you what we can afford as a family," he whispered, pulling his chair over to the end of the long table and farther from the old people.

"But if—" She turned her face away a little bit and scooched her chair around to the very end of the table, too, pulling her plate after her. She lowered her voice even further. "But if Moe were to marry my grandmother, he'd be part of our family, too. And my family could pitch in."

Right. Where his couldn't.

"We don't need help," he whispered.

"That's pride, Arden." Color deepened in her cheeks. "There's no shame in accepting help, especially when it comes from a community. That's why we pull together. It's the reason behind our entire way of life—a community!"

"There's such a thing as taking care of your own business, too," he countered.

"They aren't business—they're people," she whispered. "And they deserve happiness as much as the rest of us."

"I'm not saying they don't deserve happiness," he whispered. "I'm saying that the rest of us have our own things to take care of, too."

"Like what?" she asked. "If we're willing to pay—"

"It wouldn't be you." He clenched his jaw in an effort to keep his voice low enough. "It would be your father. So stop offering his money as if it's your own."

Her eyes glittered with anger. "You have your own business to take care of, but did it ever occur to you that I might have my own, too? I've been staying with my grandmother—and I love it. I do. But I can't find a husband here. I know everyone, and I've gone through my options. I need more than this, Arden. As much as I love this community and my family here, I need more if I'm going to get married and start my own family. But I can't go anywhere unless my grandmother is taken care of. And if I up and leave, she won't be able to stay in her home. But if she and Moe do truly love each other, they could stay together."

"Are you admitting that you're trying to force something between them?" he whispered.

"Force?" She shook her head. "Never! I'm observant, Arden. But your lives in Ohio aren't the only ones on the line here."

Her breath was coming quick and fast, and she put

her fork down with a clink. They stared at each other for a moment, the air between them almost crackling. Then Sarai reached out and took his plate of corn bread.

"What are you doing?" he demanded, his voice now at full volume.

"Your grandfather is eating this because he thinks it's salvageable. He honestly thinks so. You're eating it because he's eating it. I won't make you eat something that you think is ruined."

She got up from the table and carried the corn bread to the compost bin.

"Sarai—"

Arden started to stand up, but he noticed then that the old people were watching them, their mouths agape. He felt his own face flood with heat.

"I'll just—" He gestured feebly in Sarai's direction, and he saw the meaningful look in his grandfather's eyes. Arden was embarrassing the old man. *Yah*, he couldn't easily explain this. They had only heard the end of that exchange. Arden got up and headed over to where she stood in the kitchen. The rest of the corn bread was still in the skillet on the counter.

"What did I do?" he asked.

"Nothing. Your family's future depends on Moe going with you. But my future—any chance I've got—lies in Moe staying."

"Or you could just tell your grandmother how you feel…"

"I'm her ticket to freedom," Sarai said with a helpless shrug. "How can I do that? You might not believe me, but I care deeply about Mammi Ellen's happiness. And Moe's, too. I won't sacrifice them for myself."

This wasn't selfish on her part. That certainty was growing inside of him. Sarai would stay here if her grandmother didn't have someone else.

"I have a family who needs me in Ohio, too," he said softly. "I understand what it's like to put your own hopes on hold for the family. But your *mammi* doesn't expect you to stay single forever."

"No, but I'm the one who's giving her more time in her beloved house. My freedom comes at the price of hers. I do care about them. Moe is wonderful, and my *mammi* does care for him a lot. She said so."

"She does?"

"Yah."

"I'm not trying to ruin their happiness, Sarai." Arden swallowed. "Or yours. I promise you that. There's more to it that I can't explain. But I can't just come back and help my grandfather stay on his farm. He's already asked, and it's impossible, and I have more reasons than just helping my family financially in Ohio. I have to pay some debts, and I can't make enough here to do it. You'll just have to believe me."

Would she believe him? He wasn't sure. But soon enough she'd know who he owed money to, and she'd think the worst of him. He picked up a butter knife, cut a piece of corn bread from the top of the pan and popped it into his mouth.

"You don't have to do that, Arden," she said.

He chewed, thoroughly tasting the corn bread. "It's good," he said. "A little burned, *yah*, but overall very good. Just because my grandfather knows something doesn't mean I can't learn from him, does it? That's what I'm hoping to do while I'm here, anyway—learn a few things about starting a good life with a good woman."

In Ohio.

Sarai smiled faintly. "Maybe you can learn a thing or two. We do appreciate your help today, Arden."

That was the thing about Sarai: she didn't waste a compliment, and he knew she wouldn't say it if she didn't truly mean it.

"It's no problem."

"Tomorrow, my *daet* is rounding up some neighbors to help us with the coop," she said.

"I'm happy to pitch in," he said.

"Okay." She smiled then.

Arden looked over his shoulder at the table, and he cut another piece of corn bread, then nodded toward his chair.

"I'm still hungry, Sarai," he said.

"*Yah.* Go eat," she said, and she laughed and shook her head.

Arden went back to his place and picked up his spoon with his free hand. He was hungry, but he was also rather pleased. Sarai slid into her place, and they both tucked into their chili.

Dawdie Moe was right: Ellen's cooking was delicious, and the corn bread was edible. Arden realized as he ate that he'd choke down that entire pan of corn bread today for one reason: he wouldn't be the one who hurt Sarai's feelings. Not today. Let her have a few decent memories of him before her opinion fell.

"What happened back there?" Dawdie asked as they walked back toward the farmhouse. "You and Sarai were whispering something fierce. We couldn't hear it all, but you seemed to have some sort of issue."

"Are you sure you didn't hear it?" he asked.

"Well, I definitely heard about the corn bread," Dawdie said.

The rest would have been harder to explain.

"Sarai is giving me a few tips on how to get a good Amish girl to see more in me," he said. And she was… even if indirectly. She was showing him what she expected, and her bar was high.

"Ah." Dawdie smiled faintly.

"What do you mean, *ah*?" Arden asked.

"Are you sure she isn't showing you the way to prove yourself to her?" Dawdie asked.

Arden shook his head. The scruff grass brushed against his pant legs as they made their way between the two houses.

"She wants to find a husband in Shipshewana," he said.

"You might want to head out to Shipshewana, then," Dawdie said, and then he laughed good-naturedly.

"Dawdie, this is serious."

"Whatever happens between a young man and a young woman always is," his grandfather replied. "But mark my words, dear boy. A woman can only give you one map—and that is the map to her own heart."

Arden was silent, and the grasshoppers sprang out of the grass as they walked, launching themselves out of the way.

"One day you'll get married," Dawdie said, "and you'll hurt your wife's feelings somehow. It happens. Even between me and your grandmother. But you'll ask another woman how to make it up to your wife. Maybe you'll ask your mother or a cousin or an aunt… and they'll give you some good ideas. They'll say to bring her flowers or some new fabric to sew with or some doughnuts from the bakery. But the ideas they suggest will only be what would work to smooth their hearts over. You'll learn very quickly that you can't get advice from someone else about your own marriage."

"I'm not married yet," Arden said.

"Not yet," Dawdie said. "And I'm not saying you shouldn't listen to every word Sarai says on the subject. But keep in mind, the advice she gives is the key to her heart, and hers alone."

"She's the kind of woman I want to build a life with," Arden said. "And in the past I pursued the wrong type. I need a woman like her, with character, moral standards, intelligence and a soft heart. And that kind of woman won't respond to me flirting or playing games."

"True…"

"I've turned a new leaf," Arden said. "And I'm going to have to approach romance differently, too. What worked before isn't going to work for what I'm doing now."

"I fully agree," his grandfather said.

They came up to the familiar little house with its white paint curling and peeling around the windows, and the bushy clumps of rhubarb that had grown next to the side door. Arden waited as Dawdie made his way up the stairs slowly. He followed his grandfather into the house. When Arden shut the door behind them, Dawdie looked over at Arden thoughtfully.

"And what did you learn from Sarai today?"

"That she requires an honest compliment," he replied.

Dawdie tapped the side of his nose and headed into the kitchen, humming a little tune to himself.

"What does that mean?" he called after his grandfather.

"Just keep it in mind," Dawdie called back cheerfully. "I have a feeling it will be rather important if you want to convince Sarai to marry you!"

Arden gritted his teeth. Was his grandfather being willfully blind here? He wasn't trying to marry Sarai! He couldn't marry Sarai... He'd wronged Job five years ago by completely destroying his brand-new buggy. Job didn't know he was the culprit—no one did—and marrying the man's daughter wasn't going to make anything right, not with Gott, and not with the Peachys. First he had to pay the man back, and then he could ask Gott to bless his next steps. But not until he'd made things right.

Chapter Seven

That night, Sarai stood at the counter sorting eggs into their cartons. The hens hadn't stopped laying, after all. Sarai had found eggs in the roofless henhouse, and she'd collected them all as the sun sank down below the horizon. She'd piled them in the mesh baskets and brought them inside to be washed and sorted.

The henhouse was covered with a tarp for the moment—the best that could be done safely until it would be fixed the next day. She paused at the window. The earlier plan of setting the roof back onto the structure hadn't worked, and the blue tarp almost disappeared into the darkness. She couldn't see far, and the light of the kerosene lantern reflected off the window, showing her an image of herself with her white *kapp* and her pale face.

Upstairs, Sarai heard the sound of water running as Mammi got ready for bed, and she breathed out a soft sigh.

She'd been thinking about her conversation with Arden at supper, and her conscience had started to prick her. Was she no better than Arden, whose family was bringing Moe home so that they could be more comfortable while caring for him? Because if Mammi Ellen and Moe got married, it would benefit Sarai. But she wasn't using them. She truly wanted to see them happy.

And yet she couldn't help but wonder if her own motives were as pure as they should be. A good deed—like matchmaking a couple—should be done for the good of the couple alone.

Gott, I don't want to be selfish in this. If You want Mammi Ellen and Moe to be together, then show them what they mean to each other. I think they'd be happy together, but if I'm wrong, then I will stay here with Mammi. I'll continue to take care of her and trust You to bring me my husband.

She rinsed off two dark copper eggs and laid them on a towel to dry, then reached for some green eggs and a solitary pink one.

Mammi would be just fine with Moe at her side. Mammi could still scour a kitchen, whip up a meal and mend a hem. And she could still listen to an old man's stories with a sparkle in her eye, even though she'd heard all those stories a hundred times.

And it was Sarai's turn to begin that kind of life for herself, too…with a man her own age and children of her own to love. Sarai deserved that kind of domestic happiness just as much as Mammi did, and she didn't think it was selfish to admit it. Although, it would be selfish to use others to achieve it.

Sarai's friend Verna had been left on the tree, as they put it. Their community called unmarried women *good apples*—those too high in the branches to easily reach, so they got left there. Sarai didn't like the term: it was an attempt to soften something that couldn't be softened, and she didn't want to end up single and alone like Verna had. It wasn't fair, and Sarai knew how deeply Verna longed for her own family to love. But longing for something and having it materialize were two different things, weren't they?

Sometimes a woman had to take matters into her own hands. Verna had. She was now teaching a knitting class for at-risk Englisher youth. It might not give her many marriage opportunities, but it had opened up her life. Maybe Sarai needed to take a step of her own.

Is this a time when I'm supposed to be still and know that You are Gott, Sarai silently prayed, *or should I be dipping my foot into the Jordan and stepping forward in faith?*

Because if Sarai were honest, she wanted marching orders from Above! She wanted to do something, to make something happen for herself. Sitting around and waiting was too hard.

And yet, somehow, in the middle of her mental image of what her future could be like if she just went to Shipshewana, she found herself thinking about Arden Stoltzfus.

She irritably pulled down a carton and started to fill it. Six copper eggs, two pink and four green. Outside, the hens started to cluck and squawk, and Sarai leaned closer to the window again to look. The kerfuffle subsided, and she grabbed another cardboard carton.

Arden was proving to be hard for her to brush off. She knew the kind of man he used to be, but now that he was back, she had to admit he was different. He was more mature, for one. And he hadn't flirted with any girls yet—not that she'd seen, at least.

Three pink eggs, three blue and six green. The arrangement was pretty, and she closed the carton and stacked it, her hands doing the work without much thought.

Arden might be charming and handsome and very close by, but she had to keep her mind firm. He was also Arden Stoltzfus, the man who'd charmed his way into every heart that would let him. And Sarai was not a woman to be part of a flock. When she gave her heart, it would be to a man who saw her and only her. He didn't have to be stunningly handsome or rich or silver-tongued. What she wanted was rock-solid character and undivided loyalty. She'd be happy for the rest of her life with just that.

The hens started to squawk again, and when Sarai pushed the window open on its hinges, she heard flapping, too. This was no longer just the birds settling to sleep. Something was upsetting the hens…and she had a suspicion what it was.

She hurried over to the cupboard, stepped on a stool and grabbed the pellet air rifle from the top shelf along with an already loaded ten-shot cartridge. This wasn't the first time some animal had come prowling after her hens, and it wouldn't be the last. She loaded the cartridge and slipped the second filled cartridge into the bib of her apron.

The problem with coyotes was that a loud noise might scare them off, but they'd come back. What sent them into the trees for good was a pellet to the hindquarters. That kind of a sting would teach them a lesson and make them a little less willing to come snooping after the hens.

She slipped out the side door and raised the rifle to her shoulder. Her feet were bare, and the grass was cool against the bottoms of her feet as she crept forward. She saw movement by the coop—a tail disappearing around the side of the building, and the hens went up into a flap again.

If the windstorm hadn't made them stop laying but some coyotes did, Sarai was going to be really annoyed.

Another coyote could be seen by the fence, eyes glowing green in the light from the kitchen window. Sarai looked down the barrel and squeezed the trigger. There was the soft pop of air as the pellet left the gun, and then a yip from the coyote as it turned tail and ran.

"One," she whispered.

Another coyote came running across the yard—dangerously close—and she followed it with the rifle, then pulled the trigger. *Pop.* It didn't hit. *Pop.* That one did, and the coyote jumped and took off.

"Two."

The coyote that had circled the coop came out the other side, and she aimed once more, and it was then she heard the snap of a twig behind her. The coyote froze, and so did Sarai. She squeezed the trigger, and before she even saw if she shot true or not, she whipped around.

Standing there, his eyes as wide as the coyote's, was Arden. He wore his straw hat a little crooked on his head, and he slowly raised his hands.

"It's me," he said. "Don't shoot."

"Oh…" She lowered the rifle and laughed uncomfortably. "Did I get him?"

She turned around, and the coyote was gone.

"*Yah*, you got him. He jumped and took off," Arden said.

Sarai's heartbeat was slowing back down again. "I thought I had another coyote sneaking up on me. They work in packs, you know."

She turned again and scanned the property. She could see one coyote disappearing into the darkness, and she headed around the coop. There were scratch marks on the ground by the fence, but it looked like the predators were gone.

"I heard the chickens squawking, and I came to see if you needed help," he said, his gaze dropping to the air rifle in her hands. "But I can see you've got it under control."

Sarai chuckled. "I'm nothing if not prepared. This happens pretty often. The coyotes are plentiful out here, and I don't intend to let them get my chickens."

Arden looked around the coop, then out into the night. He turned around, seemingly satisfied.

"*Danke* for not shooting me," he said.

She laughed. "You're very welcome."

"You're a good shot." One side of his lips turned up. "I'm impressed."

"I've had lots of practice." But his compliment warmed her. "Do you want a glass of lemonade or something?"

Arden looked down at her, and suddenly she was aware just how alone they were out here in the square of light cast from the kitchen window. Arden's expression had softened, and she felt her stomach tumble in response. She didn't want to feel this way—not about Arden. He was too much of a risk for Sarai. She had plans!

"My *dawdie* is already in bed for the night," Arden said. "I wouldn't turn down something cold to drink."

"Then come on in, and I'll mix something up," she said. "I feel like I owe you something decent after that corn bread tonight."

Arden's smile broke into soft laughter, and she didn't wait to see what he'd say. Leaning the air rifle over her shoulder, Sarai turned and led the way up the steps and into the house.

Shipshewana should be her focus, but in the soft night air, Shipshewana felt very far away. And Arden Stoltzfus felt very close.

Sarai Peachy was downright impressive. At least that was all Arden could think as he followed her into the house.

She paused in the mudroom, reloaded the pellet gun and then headed into the kitchen and laid it across the counter. Eggs waited in mesh baskets on the counter, and there was a small stack of cartons to one side.

"You were busy," Arden said.

"It's tomorrow's work, actually," she said. "I was just getting a start because I wasn't ready for bed yet."

The kitchen was well stocked. He noticed the tall jars of flour on the top of some cupboards and two large gunnysacks filled with what he guessed were potatoes and possibly onions leaning against one wall. There were glass jars of dried fruit, chocolate chips and nuts lining the back of one counter—delicacies that cost quite a bit. He knew that because his mother didn't use dried fruit in her baking anymore, and when she used nuts, they were measured out carefully. He'd been grocery shopping with her, and he'd seen the prices and watched her pick up a package and put it back again.

"Pecans don't make the pie," she would say cheerfully.

Mamm made pecan pie for his birthday and then never again for a full year.

Sarai pulled down a juice pitcher, three lemons and a jar of white sugar. She worked quickly, cutting, juicing, squeezing the lemons, and mixing it all up with water and sugar. Then she poured two tall glasses and handed him one.

He took a sip. It was the perfect mix of tart and sweet.

"Should we sit on the porch?" she asked. "I don't want to wake up my grandmother."

"*Yah*, that would be nice."

Sarai picked up the air rifle and tucked it under one arm.

"In case the coyotes come back," she said, casting a smile over her shoulder.

He followed her through the sitting room. It was large enough to hold a small prayer service, and the hardwood floor shone with a recent polishing. There were two couches in the room, a large rag rug in the center, an unlit woodstove in the center of the wall shared with the kitchen, and a basket of knitting supplies sitting on the seat of a wooden rocking chair. Two big windows were cranked open to the porch outside, letting in a cool breeze.

Sarai led the way out. The porch was broad and spacious, and a wooden swing hung on one side. It was the only seating available, so Sarai leaned her air rifle against the side of the house, and they sat down, glasses of lemonade in hand. They began to gently swing. From the backyard, Arden could make out the soft contented clucking sounds from the coop.

Sarai took a sip of her lemonade and sighed softly.

"You're tougher than I thought," he said.

She looked over in surprise. "Am I?"

"Definitely."

She laughed. "Good. I like to surprise people."

"You're a good shot, too," he said. "What do you practice on?"

"Tin cans, old apples, anything small enough to be a challenge and that Mammi won't mind me filling with holes," she said.

She was definitely tougher than he'd given her credit for. "Well, it paid off."

"You're not quite what I thought you'd be, either," she said.

"Yah?"

"You've matured." She looked at him thoughtfully.

"Danke. It's nice to hear. Am I not half the fool I used to be?" he asked with a short laugh. He meant to sound cool and joking, but he cared about her answer.

"You don't seem to be."

He drank half the glass of lemonade and then put it down on the ground.

"Arden, can I ask you something?" she asked.

"Yah, of course."

"What is keeping you away from Redemption? I mean, really. Sure, you were a questionable youth, but you're a grown man now. I don't understand why you'd like yourself so much better in Ohio. It shouldn't matter."

He looked out across the dark lawn, illuminated by the light coming from inside the house, a golden glow on the grass. He hadn't told anyone this, not even his parents. When he looked over at Sarai, all he could see were those blue questioning eyes and her lips parted ever so little…

"I…did some things that I regret," he said. "And I don't like the memories."

"The flirting?" Sarai looked at him earnestly. Was that the worst she could think of?

"That, too." He smiled wanly. "Look, I did a lot of things I regret, but some things you can't undo. You can't fix them. And I won't be able to come back until I can fix it."

"Fix what?" She frowned. "Lizzie's married. I don't think she picked a terribly good man, but she's got a family of her own now. Most of the other girls whose hearts you broke are married or courting, too. If you think you're that unforgettable, Arden Stoltzfus—" There was the glitter of humor in her eyes.

"It's not that." He sighed. "Okay. You're a woman of your word, aren't you?"

"Of course."

"If I tell you something, will you promise to keep it a secret?" he said.

"Tell me what?" she asked.

"Promise you'll keep it between us first," he said.

"Okay, I promise. As long as it doesn't hurt anyone."

"It doesn't. Not anymore. But it'll explain my position, at least."

"Okay, I promise." She regarded him soberly, and their swinging stopped.

Arden exhaled a slow breath. He had become a very private man over the years. He wasn't used to sharing these things, but there was something about Sarai that was different. He trusted her promise, for one. Her honesty was a part of her. But not only that. He was ready to say something, to get this secret out into the open air. Maybe it wouldn't feel so big when he said it out loud.

"A few months before we moved away, I was hanging out with some Englisher guy at the Klassen farm," he said. The Klassens were a Mennonite family, so they were outsiders, but not quite so far as other Englishers. Still, they were a source of television and internet before he was baptized. "I knew we were moving, and I was having a lot of mixed-up feelings to do with that. I was upset with my parents for dragging me to a whole new state. I didn't yet see the gift they were giving me."

"Hmm?" Her voice was soft and encouraging.

"Abram Yoder was supposed to give me a ride home, but he'd left early, and I figured I'd walk. Or maybe Mike Klassen would give me a ride in his truck."

"*Yah*, go on." She started them swinging again.

"So we were hanging out and talking, and when it got late, I asked Mike to drive me home. We were passing the Swarey farm, and I saw this buggy—hitched up and just standing there empty. It was late. No one was around. And Mike wanted to know if I could drive a buggy at the Englisher speed limit. It was a stupid question. Of course I could, but only if the horse was running full speed, and he said he'd bet me a hundred dollars that I couldn't."

Arden pulled off his hat and ran a hand through his hair. "I was feeling rebellious and angry and...I did something stupid. I fully intended to return that buggy. But it was so much nicer than any buggy I could afford. I got a secondhand buggy when I bought my own, and it was forever having problems. I wasn't going to take that beautiful one for long. I just wanted to see how fast it could go. And prove to Mike we could match their speed limit."

"Oh, no…" she breathed.

"Yah."

"Was that my *daet*'s new buggy you took for a joyride?" she whispered.

"Yah, it was," he said, and he felt his face heat. "I'm ashamed to say it. But I took that buggy and whipped the horse up and took it down the road as fast as lightning. It was faster than I thought it would be. It was what a decent one drove like, and it felt amazing. But then I lost control, and the horse threw the buggy. Thankfully, the horse was fine. I was tossed clear of it and only suffered a few bruises. But the buggy—"

"Was ruined," she said. "It was demolished."

"So I made sure the horse was okay, and we brought it back to the Swarey place, and then I jumped into the truck, and we sped off," he said. "I fully expected to be found out, but no one ever said anything."

"We thought an Englisher had played a trick while we were at the Swareys' place," she said. "We heard the truck."

"It was me." He swallowed. "I have some of the money to pay your *daet* back for the damage I did. I'm going to give it to him before I leave for home, and I will come back, Sarai. I will. But when I come back, it will be to hand over the rest of the cash to him to buy a brand-new buggy to replace the one I ruined. And not before."

"He'd forgive you, if you told him it was you," she said. "He won't make you repay it."

"He might forgive me, but he'd never respect me," he replied. "No, I will do it right or not at all."

"How much have you got saved up?" she asked.

"About half of what I'd need," he said. "The irony is we moved out to Ohio, and every penny I made, my family has needed for some emergency or other. If we're not fixing a buggy or paying for medical bills, then we're fixing the plumbing or replacing a roof. It's constant."

"If you came back alone, saving might be easier."

"Can Gott really bless the easier path?" he asked. "My family needs me, too, and I pray constantly that He will provide a way for me to get the money I owe your father. I won't come back the easy way, and I won't face your *daet* with this until I can do it as a man with the money to pay him back."

"You were thinking of getting married, though—" Sarai said. "To Mary."

"I thought I could just tell Gott I was sorry and put it behind me," he admitted. "It was cowardly on my part, and Gott didn't bless that, did He?"

"No. I suppose not."

"When a man messes up, he has to make it right, Sarai," he said quietly. "There is an apology, confession, Gott's forgiveness, your brother's forgiveness, and then making it right again. But I have to do it properly. I'm going to pay him back for the buggy I totaled."

"You really have grown up," she murmured.

He met her gaze. "Enough to know when I'm well and truly wrong about something."

"I think you're being very noble," she said, and her voice trembled.

He reached for her hand before he could think better of it, and instead of pushing him away, she closed her fingers around his.

"If you feel that you have to tell your *daet*—" he started.

"I don't. The accident was forgotten a long time ago. Daet has never spoken of it since. But I can appreciate you wanting to make it right in a way my father can respect."

"Danke." He squeezed her hand. "I've never told a living person that before."

"No one?" Her eyes widened.

"No one." He swallowed. What had he just done? He'd just told his deepest secret to the daughter of the man he'd wronged... He shut his eyes. He really was a fool! And when he opened them again, he found Sarai still looking at him.

"Why did you tell me?" she whispered.

"You're different." He reached out and touched her cheek. "I don't know how. Maybe you're just everything I want one day—once I finally deserve it."

Sitting here in the low kerosene light coming from the window, she looked prettier than he'd ever seen a woman look. Her eyes were like pools, tugging him in, but he wouldn't let himself go.

"I think..." She licked her lips and dropped her gaze. "I think you're a decent man after all, Arden."

He felt a rush of gratitude, but then he heard the slippered footfalls of Mammi Ellen through the open window.

"Are you outside, Sarai?" Ellen called.

Color suddenly bloomed in Sarai's cheeks, and she pulled her hand out of his. "*Yah*, Mammi! I'm just talking with Arden."

Mammi came to the open window. She was dressed in a big bathrobe, a handkerchief over her hair.

"Well, Arden, I think it's time you headed on home, don't you? Sarai, it's late."

Arden didn't need to be chased off the porch for the point to be made. And Ellen was right. It was high time he headed back to his grandfather's house, before he did something he'd regret, like kiss Sarai out here in the soft light.

"*Yah*, I'll be going." He picked up the glass on the ground and then handed it to Sarai, and she picked up the gun and tucked it under her arm again. Then he headed for the stairs that led down to the grass. "Good night, Sarai and Ellen."

"Good night, Arden," Sarai said. Her hands were full with two glasses and the air rifle squeezed between her arm and her side. Her grandmother took the glasses from her, and they turned away from him.

As Arden walked away, he could make out the quiet voices of Sarai and Ellen talking to each other, then the clatter of the screen and the thump of the front door. When he looked over his shoulder, the porch was empty, the door was shut, and then the light from inside winked out.

Sarai really was an impressive woman—and it wasn't just her way around a pellet gun, either. She was different from any other woman he'd ever known. And she thought he was downright decent. Even when he'd told her his worst... He couldn't help grinning all the way back to his grandfather's house.

One day he'd repay her father the full amount, and she'd know he'd kept his word. She'd probably be married to some other, much worthier man, but he wanted her to know it all the same.

Chapter Eight

The next morning, Sarai finished washing and packing the last of the eggs. Her customers came by early, picking up their orders, and she had a few more Englishers stop and ask if she had any extras for sale. There were a few, and by the time buggies started to arrive for the coop raising, laden with tools and helpful friends, the eggs were all sold, and she'd sent two hopeful customers away empty-handed.

Sarai's mind was on Arden, though, and their time together on the porch. He'd been so open, so gentle. She'd never seen that side to him before, and she'd felt like the only person in his whole world on that porch swing.

Had he truly changed? She wasn't sure…but she'd meant it when she told him he'd matured into a decent man. If he was so determined to pay her *daet* back, she couldn't help but be swayed…

Sarai's parents arrived first in their buggy. Job and Esther came into the house carrying supplies in bags and a big wooden crate her father held in one strong arm.

"Mamm, how are you doing?" Job asked, sliding the crate onto the table.

"Oh, just fine, Job," Mammi replied. "We had a nice cool breeze coming through the upstairs windows last night, so we slept wonderfully."

"Sarai, how is Arden doing?" Esther asked, piling some grocery items onto the counter. "I know he's been back for a few days. Everyone has been talking about it."

"Oh, he's doing well," Sarai said. And she felt her face warm as she remembered the feeling of his strong hand on hers.

"She's been spending some time with him, actually," Mammi said with a little smile.

"Have you?" Esther looked at Sarai curiously. "I suppose you have some memories together from youth group."

"A few," Sarai hedged.

"What's he like now?" her mother asked.

"He's..." Sarai frowned, wondering how to explain him. "He's turned out to be quite decent, I think."

"In spite of everything? I'm glad. That boy was on more than one prayer list, I can assure you." Esther turned back to the groceries and started putting them away. "His parents did their very best, but there comes a point when every child has to choose who they'll be."

"I didn't know that you parents discussed us," Sarai said.

"Well, we weren't about to give you *kinner* things to gossip over, were we?" Esther asked. "I'm sure you were on several prayer lists, too. A community prays over their young people. You are our future, after all. But Arden's *mamm* often asked us to pray for her son.

When he wouldn't listen to them, she asked us to pray for someone to be placed in his path who he would listen to."

Sarai helped her mother put away some groceries, and the conversation turned to the windstorm damage and the plans for the day. Another buggy pulled in, and Sarai went to the door and saw Verna driving up with her niece, Susie, sitting next to her in the open seat. Verna waved, and Sarai headed outside to say hello.

More folks arrived: Claire and Joel with their five-year-old son, and Adel and Jake Knussli with their toddler, too. Just as Adel and Jake drove up, Sarai saw Arden and Moe coming across the field toward them. With this many hands, the work would go fast, and Sarai was grateful for a supportive community at a time like this. But her gaze kept moving back toward Arden. He looked a little shy, hanging back a bit behind his grandfather, and she felt a pang of sympathy for him. Coming back wasn't easy.

"Sarai!" Verna called from her seat in the buggy as she reined in the horse. "Your *daet* told us that the storm hit here worst."

"*Yah*, it sure seemed to." Sarai headed over, and her friend jumped down to the ground.

"You remember Susie?" Verna said.

Susie was young, plump and pretty. She smiled and put her hands on her hips, looking around. At seventeen, she was on her *Rumspringa* and had come from another community to stay with her aunt and grandparents.

"Hi, Susie," Sarai said. "Thanks for coming to help."

"Of course I'd come," Susie said, and she looked over

in the direction of Arden and Moe, who were still approaching. "Who's he?"

"That's our neighbor Moe," Sarai said, "and his grandson."

"Is he single?" Susie asked with a smile.

"Moe? Yes, but he's got grandchildren older than you, Susie," Verna joked. "Come on, now. You're here to help, not flirt."

"Very funny. You know who I meant. I was just asking," Susie said, and she leaned over to get a better look at Arden again. "He's awfully handsome, isn't he?"

Sarai felt a little tremor of jealousy at the way the girl was gawking at Arden, and she did her best to tamp it down. That was the way things always were with Arden. Girls stared.

"Have you no shame?" Verna said. "Stop staring like that!"

"I'm just looking."

"Arden is too old for you, too," Sarai added. "Trust me on that. There's lots of time to find a nice boy."

"Sometimes you stumble upon them, though," Susie said with a twinkle in her eye. "Can you introduce me?"

"Go bring the cookies inside, would you?" Verna said tersely. "I'll unhitch."

"Is that a *yes* or a *no*?" Susie asked, her smile slipping and a petulant look coming to her face.

"That's a *no*, young lady," Verna replied. "Come on, now. Bring the cookies inside. Unless you'd rather wrangle the horse."

"I'll take the cookies," Susie said, and with an exaggerated sigh she headed toward the house, taking a large plastic container out of the back of the buggy. When she disappeared inside, Verna shook her head.

"I have to keep my eye on her," Verna said. "She's such a flirt. She's just figured out that she's pretty, and all she can think of is how her dress fits or if boys are single. You'd think she was one of my Englisher at-risk girls at the knitting class. But even those girls are smarter than this! Mind you, they learned a lot of their lessons the hard way."

A whole lot like Arden had been at that age. Sarai set to work on the other side of the horse, unbuckling the harness.

"Is that why her parents sent her here, to smarten up a little bit?" Sarai asked.

"*Yah*. She's made a reputation for herself back home, and my brother asked me to talk to her about being more serious and sober. So far, she isn't listening to me, mostly because she doesn't want to end up like me."

"She could do far worse!" Sarai said.

"*Yah*, but she's completely boy crazy! It doesn't help that she could pass for twenty."

"That doesn't help at all," Sarai agreed.

They talked as they worked, and Sarai told her about Arden's help around the place, but she stopped short at the rest of her concerns. When they had the horse unhitched and sent out to the corral to eat, Arden came up, a tool belt slung over one shoulder.

"Hi, Verna," he said, and he gave her a polite nod.

"Arden Stoltzfus," Verna said. "Good to see you. I heard you were around."

"*Yah*, just visiting my *dawdie*."

"And helping out here, I heard," Verna said.

"Well...being neighborly." Arden's gaze caught Sarai's, and his cheeks colored just a bit. "She almost shot me last night."

"I did not!" Sarai laughed. "If you had been a coyote, that would have been a different story."

"She's a very good shot," Arden said to Verna. "She'd put me to shame on a hunting trip."

"I only shoot pellets," Sarai said. "I don't want to shoot a big gun. They're too heavy, and I think the hunting and cleaning is a job for the men."

"I couldn't agree more," Verna said. "It takes a stronger stomach than I've got. But the coyotes were out?"

"*Yah*, coming after my coop," Sarai said. "I'll be glad when it's solid again."

The men came out of the house then, and Arden nodded in their direction. "I'd better get to work. See you. Nice seeing you again, Verna. Talk to you later, Sarai."

Arden smiled at Sarai and headed in the direction of the coop. Her father was out there, as well as Jake, Joel and Moe. Arden strolled up and stood with his weight on one leg, the tool belt hanging over his shoulder. He always had stood out in a group of men, and Sarai hated how her eyes seemed to be magnetically attracted to him. And it wasn't just his good looks, either. Arden was softer and gentler than he'd been before. And more vulnerable.

Verna leaned closer to Sarai. "He likes you."

"I know," she said dismally. She knew he liked her, but what did that mean? Was she just the last in a long line of women he'd already left in weepy heaps behind him? Was she a challenge to conquer? He said he wanted to win a woman like her... Was he proving something to himself?

"So if you know he likes you..." Verna gave her a curious look. "Do you like him?"

Yes. Immensely. Dangerously! She shouldn't like him as much as she did.

"You remember Arden from before," Sarai said. "He was a flirt. Can you imagine being married to a man who made girls giggle everywhere he went? That's not a life for me."

"No, I agree with you," Verna replied. "Is he still like that?"

She had no idea. "I think he's grown up a lot. He's matured in other ways. He wants to be more serious."

"But...?" Verna prompted.

"But he's a risk," Sarai said with a shrug. "Everyone has more than one side to them, and I've seen the other side to Arden. I've seen a sweet, uncertain part of him that wants to be better."

"My knitting class wants to be better," Verna said softly. "That's what makes me so protective of them. They have had such hard starts in life, and they want so badly to set things right, and they don't know how."

"Arden got a perfectly fine start in life," Sarai said.

"I know. But figuring out how to walk straight when you've been doing otherwise can still be a challenge. It takes... I don't know. It takes determination and a true change of habits. That's not easy."

"That's my worry, exactly."

The women were silent for a moment, and Sarai sighed. Was she no better than Lizzie or the other girls who used to swoon for this man? Was she just being foolish now that he'd focused that smile of his on her? Or was she right, and Ohio had truly changed him?

"Sarai!" Job called. "We'll need you to get your chickens into another pen for now, okay?"

"*Yah*, Daet!" she called back, and she shot her friend a smile. "Enough about Arden. This is where I need your help. Are you up to chasing chickens?"

"Of course!" Verna said.

The women came outside then, and they all gathered hens up into their arms and brought them over to a makeshift pen. Adel and Verna got one chicken each, but Mammi was an old hand at this and had one under each arm. A few got feisty and made a flapping, hopping run for it, and Sarai went after the escaping birds. Her mother helped her to corral one of them beside a pile of fresh lumber.

"Got it!" Sarai scooped up her hen and shook her head. "You'll have to settle down, Red. You'll be glad of this new coop, I promise you that."

Then she handed Red off to her mother and went after the next one on the loose that she'd named Dusty Girl. Dusty fluttered up into a bush, and Sarai got her arm scratched as she caught her by the legs and pulled her safely against her apron.

She looked over to where the women were putting the birds into the pen, and Verna and Adel were laughing over a runaway they'd managed to track down. Mammi stood with her hands on her hips, giving orders to keep the hens calm.

"No one wins with flustered poultry!" Mammi said. "If you stay calm, they will, too."

That wasn't entirely true, but it worked in many cases,

at least. It was then that Sarai spotted Susie. She wasn't helping chase chickens with everyone else. Instead, she stood a few yards away next to Arden. She was blushing and looking up at him bashfully. Arden was smiling at something, and he shrugged. Susie reached out and batted his arm. He just shrugged again, but then he looked down at her, and she could see Susie just melt under his gaze.

And despite Sarai's indignation, she couldn't really blame a seventeen-year-old girl for swooning over Arden's good looks. Many a girl before her had done the same. Suddenly, it all seemed so clear to Sarai that it felt like a kick in the stomach. Arden was Arden. He always would be. She was the fool who was hoping to see more in the man because it felt so wonderful to have him look at *her* the way he did. But that didn't make her special. In fact, she probably owed her cousin a sincere apology for having gotten so exasperated with her tears.

She tucked Dusty Girl under her arm and headed back toward the pen. But she felt a heaviness inside of her that hadn't been there before.

"I'm going to Shipshewana," she reminded herself. "Just as soon as I can manage it."

But even Shipshewana wasn't the comfort it had been in the past, and she wished she knew why.

Gott, keep my head on straight! she prayed.

Arden shifted his feet uncomfortably. Susie had latched on to him, and he wasn't sure how to get rid of her. She was a pretty girl, but very young. Somehow, she'd learned his name and was chatting with him like an equal in age, when she was nothing of the sort. She wasn't even old enough to understand the hints that he wasn't interested. Susie nudged his arm again.

"So do you have a girlfriend, Arden?" she asked.

So forward! He couldn't believe she was doing this. Wasn't someone supposed to be keeping an eye on her?

"You don't have to worry about that," Arden said, shaking his head.

"No?" She sidled closer.

What message had she just gotten from what he'd said? He was trying to tell her that she was too young and he was not interested, which was why his relationship status was none of her business, but she didn't seem to be getting that from him. He also didn't want to hurt her feelings. She was just a kid, really. All of seventeen and just starting her *Rumspringa*—that time of freedom that teenagers enjoyed before they got serious about things. He knew all of this because she'd told him all about herself while he stood here, trapped by politeness. She thought she was grown-up enough to talk to single men, and maybe he could sympathize with teenage hubris. He'd felt so old and mature at that age, too. He most certainly wasn't, though. He'd acted like a fool. Much like Susie was right now.

"Susie, I'm not someone you should be interested in. I'm sure you'll meet plenty of young people your age at the youth group if you stay long enough," he said.

"I might…" She shrugged. "Maybe you could take me driving sometime. I'd really like that."

That was even more forward, and he looked down at her in shock. She smiled sweetly.

"Oh, you think I'm trying to ask you on a date!" She tittered. "No, silly! I just wanted a ride. I have my own little open-top buggy at home, but I don't have it here. I miss the freedom."

That was a thinly veiled excuse. There were buggies at her disposal at her aunt and uncle's place.

"I don't think your *daet* would like it," he said. Maybe he could remind her of her father's expectations of her. That might sober the girl up.

"My *daet*'s not here. They sent me out to Redemption to get to know my grandparents better."

"Then your grandfather," he amended.

"He won't mind." She smiled up at him. "I'd like to just get out for a little bit and talk. I get so bored with my aunt and my grandmother all the time. They're so prim and proper."

"You should be prim and proper, too," he said. "That's probably the hope, you know."

"No, I shouldn't!" she said, laughing. "What fun would that be? You're just teasing now."

He smiled ruefully. She was such a kid! He had a younger sister her age, and he fully intended to tell his sister this story as a bit of a warning tale.

"Arden, we could be friends," Susie said. "We could talk… You could even write to me. That's very proper, isn't it?" She slipped a piece of paper into his hand, and Arden felt his own face heat. He crunched it into a ball in his palm. No, he was not writing to this girl, and he hated how she was embarrassing herself.

Except he was the one who was embarrassed, and she seemed perfectly comfortable.

"Susie, you should go help the women," he said firmly.

Arden looked over toward the pen, and he spotted

Sarai looking at him, a displeased set to her lips. Standing next to her was Verna, Susie's aunt. Verna's eyes snapped fire, and she left Sarai's side and stalked toward him.

His first instinct was to take a step back, but he was actually relieved that she was coming over. She could take her niece in hand.

"Susie, what are you doing?" Verna asked briskly as she strode up.

"Talking." Susie's tone took on a decidedly defiant cast.

"We need help with the chickens," Verna said.

"You seem to have it under control," Susie replied.

Verna planted her hands on her hips and met the girl's gaze. "Now."

Susie sighed, then cast Arden a bright smile. "See you, Arden."

He wasn't sure what to say, so he opted for silence as Susie headed over to where the other women were still rounding up the last of the chickens. Verna didn't move, and she gave him an annoyed look.

"She is far too young for you, Arden," Verna said.

"I know! I know… I just… I mean… She, um—" How on earth was he supposed to explain what had just happened here? That little ball of paper seemed to be burning a hole in his palm.

"She's seventeen. Barely seventeen," Verna said. "And she has a lot to learn before she's wife material for anyone. If you think you're interested in a girl that young, then I think you need to have a talk with some elders! But I'll tell you this much. You'd have to wait several years for her to be old enough for anything serious!"

"I'm not! I—" Arden swallowed.

"Arden, I remember you very well from your younger years," Verna said, lowering her voice. "Very well. And my niece might be foolish enough to want to play with these things, but I've got my eye on her, and you'd better keep your distance. I'm serious."

"Verna, I promise you, I'm not interested in Susie," he said. "I'm not in Redemption for that. She's just... very friendly, it seems."

"Friendly." Verna rolled her eyes. She didn't seem ready to forgive him yet.

"Trust me." He needed to get away from here—and he didn't deserve this lecture from Verna. He hadn't done anything wrong.

"If you're thinking about finding a wife, I suggest you stick to the women closer to your own age," Verna said. "My advice? Sarai Peachy is beautiful, smart and single. That would be more fruitful than flirting with a girl Susie's age."

"I wasn't flirting!" he said.

Susie had been, and shamelessly, but he hadn't been. That was the honest truth, not that Verna looked inclined to believe him. But then her advice landed a couple of beats after she said it. "Wait—why would you say Sarai?"

"Because she's closer to your age," Verna said.

"But she's not interested in a man like me," he said. "Her family is significantly better-off than mine, and when she gets married, it'll be to someone who can give her some proper comfort. I'm downright poor next to her family, you know."

Verna cocked her head to one side, and a smile tickled her lips. "Do you think that she's a step above you?"

"She's several steps above me, Verna," he said. "That's a fact."

"Maybe she is." But that smile didn't leave Verna's lips. "All the same, you're better-off barking up that tree than socializing with my niece. Consider Sarai a challenge."

Sarai would be a challenge, indeed. But he didn't need any encouragement in that direction.

"I'm not staying long," he said. "And I'm not looking for romance of any kind. Maybe you could make that clear to Susie."

"I'll try," Verna said. "I'm not sure she'll listen, but I'll do my best."

"Danke," he said. "I appreciate that."

The men had moved into a circle and were discussing their building plans. That was Arden's cue to go join them.

"I need to go help," he said.

"Go on, then," Verna said.

Arden headed toward the group of men, and he looked back in Sarai's direction. She wasn't watching him anymore. Her attention was on the hens and making sure they had proper feed and water. She was petting one of them, crouching next to it comfortingly.

He'd have to stop thinking about Sarai, too, because contrary to Verna's opinion, he had no future here in Redemption. If Gott wanted him back here, He'd have provided the full sum of money to pay Job back. And He hadn't. That was a clear-enough message.

He looked down at the paper in his palm. He flattened it and looked at the writing neatly printed in blue ink. It was Susie's name and address. He shut his eyes for a moment, balled the paper up again in his palm and dropped it into his tool bag. He'd dispose of it later. But that would be a difficult one to explain to Sarai, and he knew it.

The day melted into some hard work. Jake Knussli had a sketch done for a larger coop than the one Sarai had been using up to this point. The plans were laid out, and then Arden's job was measuring and cutting two-by-fours. He could do that easily enough, and the other men took the newly cut wood and set to work on building the new coop.

The women put together some lunch for everyone—sandwiches, stew and cut fruit. Arden ate with the men, and Sarai kept her distance. He caught her giving him a wary look now and again, and after Verna's lecture, he understood why. She thought he had been flirting. But he hadn't been, and if he could just explain himself, he'd feel a bit better. Sarai wasn't giving him a chance.

A couple of times Susie came over to where they were working, and Verna was close behind, herding her irritated niece back toward the women again. Arden couldn't help but chuckle at that.

He put himself into the work instead. He used his tape to get the exact measurement, marked it with a pencil, measured again to be sure and then pulled out his handsaw.

"I see the Kauffman niece has set her sights on you," Job said.

Arden looked up. "Not my fault, I promise you."

"*Yah*, I know." Job nodded. "How are things in Ohio?"

"They're fine." Arden pressed his lips together and leaned into the saw, blade slicing neatly through the wood as he pushed and pulled.

"Are things, really?" Job pressed. "I heard it's been tough. Really tough."

The end of the wood dropped off, and Arden wiped his calloused fingers over the cut surface. Then he looked up at Job again.

"It's been hard," he admitted. "We don't have a very big community yet, so sharing the load is...a bigger burden between fewer people."

"Understood," Job said. "What would help?"

"More people," Arden said with a short laugh.

"And until more people come?" Job wasn't joking. He met his gaze evenly. "What's the biggest need right now?"

Arden swallowed. "My *daet* needs a new thresher. We're saving, though. We'll get there."

"You need a down payment, I imagine?" Job said. "Maybe a down payment and the first few monthly payments, just to make sure there's a cushion there?"

That would be incredibly helpful, but Arden shook his head.

"Job, you'd have to discuss that with my father. I'm not the owner of our farm, if you know what I mean. That's my *daet*'s business."

"Your *daet* isn't here, and you are," Job replied. "And Gott has put it onto my heart to help your family out. I just need to know how."

"It's kind, but—" How on earth was Arden supposed to accept any kind of help from a man he already owed so much to? "I'm not the man to talk to about this, though."

"You are a man in the community," Job said.

"Yah." That couldn't be argued.

"Then straighten your shoulders, Arden," Job said with a rueful smile. "I'm discussing it with you."

"Oh." Arden swallowed and sent up a panicked little prayer. "Then I thank you for your kindness and generosity, but maybe the help you could give me is to help me bring my grandfather home. He hates the idea of leaving his farm, but he needs the extra help. He's not a young man."

"We do look in on him," Job said. "He's not on his own here in Redemption."

"Yah, but we're his family, with all due respect," Arden said. "Gott gave us community, but the first circle is family."

"Fair enough. I'll help you out wherever I can."

Job looked a little perplexed but nodded and was just turning away when Arden said, "And, Job?"

The older man turned back. *"Yah?"*

"I just want you to know that I didn't want to put that roofing material on your tab," he said. "I was going to pay it myself."

"No need, son," Job said. "That would have been a burden to you, and not fair at all."

"Yah, but it felt wrong," Arden said. "I don't presume upon other men's tabs. And I wanted you to know."

"No problem, Arden," Job said with a smile. "You and I are even. My daughter knew I'd want her to use the tab. Don't worry about it."

Except they weren't even. Not by a long shot, and as

the older man headed back over to where the building and hammering was happening, Arden wished that this conversation could make him feel better. But it didn't. Job was being kind. He was treating a young upstart like Arden as an equal, when Arden was anything but. Job wanted to help the new fledgling community, and he was in a financial position to do so. What would Arden's father say when he told him about the offer?

Likely, his *daet* wouldn't want to accept the help, either. But their farm needed more than hard work: it needed some divine intervention. Job said Gott had placed it on his heart... But why Job? he wondered helplessly. Why the one man Arden could never accept it from?

But Job was also the man who could most easily afford the gift. Gott had blessed him mightily in his farm and his finances.

If he accepted, Arden would never be truly out of debt to this man, would he?

Chapter Nine

The chicken coop was finished in a morning. With that many hands working, it came together quickly, and it stood in the same spot as the last coop, strong and straight. It had red siding so that it would never need painting and would withstand the elements. The roof was covered with high-quality shingles, and it was bigger than the first coop, too, so that Sarai could grow her flock even more.

Arden was proud of their work, and when they went home that afternoon, he felt like they'd done a good job for Sarai and Ellen. Moe stayed in Ellen's kitchen for a coffee and some chatting, but Arden went back to the farmhouse to do a few chores for his grandfather. He realized halfway back to his grandfather's house that he'd forgotten his tool bag, but he could go back for it later. He needed some space right now.

Besides, Sarai was being much cooler around him now. She gave him polite conversation, but the warmth and sparkle was gone. And with Moe and Ellen present, he couldn't exactly explain himself, could he?

Arden washed up some dishes in the sink, wiped down the cupboards and then picked up a broom. But as he did so, his gaze landed on a pile of envelopes that sat in a little letter holder next to the hook that held the broom. He'd seen them a hundred times, but today with his general feeling of frustration stewing, he reached out and picked up the tight bunch.

He pulled a sheet out of the first envelope. It was a bill. He scanned it: it was from the hardware store. Moe had several hundred dollars owing. The next was a bill, too, for the butcher. More money owing. The next one was for the buggy shop—the same again. This bill looked like it had been outstanding for a couple of years now.

Arden flipped through the envelopes. Bills, all of them. The Amish dry-goods store, the Petersheim Creamery, a veterinary clinic—that bill was by far the highest, and it came with a bold typed request that Moe pay up his bill as quickly as possible. This had come several months ago.

Arden's heart beat faster. He'd mentally tallied up the amount owing, and it was in the thousands of dollars. Arden had just enough in his savings account to cover the lot of it, but no more. He rubbed a hand over his eyes. What was he going to do?

Gott, You keep providing our daily bread and not much else. This will empty me out... You know how hard I've saved. You know I need to make things right with Job. Why does hardship keep coming?

But it did: expense after expense kept hitting him. And his carefully saved dollars—saved by doing without any extras at all—were going to be depleted this afternoon. Because he knew what he had to do. He had to square away his grandfather's debts. But then Moe would have to see reason and come back to Ohio. Moe wasn't doing okay on his own. He couldn't afford to keep the farm going. That was just a plain fact.

His grandfather was going to be embarrassed. Arden felt his heart squeeze at that thought. The old man would be humbled—and Moe was the last one who needed humbling.

Arden took the broom and swept the kitchen, his heart heavy. How on earth was he going to discuss this with his grandfather? After paying the bills, of course. That would have to be taken care of first, and then he could sit down with Moe and discuss the state of things with him. At times like this, Arden wished he weren't the only one on hand to take care of these issues. He wished there were an older man in the family to handle them for him, but there wasn't anyone else. Just like Job had pointed out, he was the man who was here, and the responsibility was his.

Arden put the broom back on its hook, pocketed the bills and headed outside to hitch up his grandfather's buggy. As he worked, he heard his name called in the distance. He looked up, shaded his eyes and spotted Ellen standing outside, waving a towel in the air.

Was something wrong? He headed in her direction, picking up his pace and breaking into a jog. When he got to her, Ellen's face was pink.

"I'm sorry to make you run, Arden," the old lady said. "I didn't mean to do that. I just wanted to get your attention. Are you going out?"

"Yah," he said. "I'm heading out to run a few errands."

"Would you be a dear and fetch my butter order for me?" she asked. "The creamery is in town, and it closes at six tonight. I need to pick it up, and if you're headed in that direction—"

"Yah, I'm happy to get it for you," he said. "I'll be in town all afternoon. It's not out of my way at all."

Sarai came out of the house, and for the first time in a few hours, she met his gaze.

"I'll come with you, Arden," Sarai said.

"Yah?" He wasn't sure what to make of her change of heart.

"We need to talk," she said, but her tone was firm, and that didn't encourage him a whole lot. He had a sneaking suspicion that she was the one who needed to talk, and he was supposed to sit and listen.

"Well, that works nicely," Ellen said with a smile. "Moe and I will enjoy our coffee, and when you two get back, I'll pull out the blackberry pie."

"Sure," Arden said, and he shot Sarai an uncertain look. "I can do it myself, you know."

"I'll come along," she said, still sounding more firm than friendly.

Right. That was clear enough. Maybe it was for the best. He wasn't going to let her lecture him. He had a few things of his own to explain. And soon enough, Moe would be telling Ellen that he was moving.

It was time to sort it all out and get back home.

"Let's go, then," he said. "I'll bring that order back for you, Ellen."

"*Danke*, Arden," Ellen said with a smile. "I appreciate it."

Arden stayed half a step ahead of Sarai as they headed back to where the horse waited, only half hitched up. He got back to work with the buckles and straps. He meant to simply ignore Sarai until she was ready to talk, but when he looked over at her, he caught her unawares, and she looked more sad than angry.

"Are you okay?" he asked.

"Not really," she replied. "I should be. It shouldn't matter. I know that, but somehow—" She swallowed.

"I wasn't flirting with Susie," he said, tightening the last strap and then straightening. "I want to say that right away. She was flirting with me, all right. But she's a kid. She's on her *Rumspringa*, and she's finally allowed to keep company with some boys. She's feeling the power of it. That's all. I know it looked bad. Verna thought the same thing, but I wasn't flirting with her. I was trying to politely send her back to you women."

Sarai eyed him. "It didn't look that way."

"I know." He shook his head. "And I know with my history, you'd assume the worst. I don't even blame you. But I wasn't doing that. What do you think—that I want to pass my time getting a teenager's hopes up? Come on, Sarai. I'm not that kind of man. Not anymore, at least. I've grown up."

Sarai eyed him for a moment, silent.

"Do you believe me?" he asked.

"I think I do." She shook her head. "I'm sorry. But you do realize that, more than just your history, you draw a lot of female attention."

"Are you calling me *handsome*?" He shot her a grin.

"No, I am not!" she said, her cheeks coloring.

"It sounded almost like that," he teased.

"Well, fine. You are handsome, and apparently you know it," she said. "And you'll always get that attention. You'll need more character than most to deal with it."

The implication seemed to be that he didn't have character in quite that supply.

"And you think you're any different?" he asked, then hoisted himself up into the buggy. "Come on."

Sarai got up next to him and settled into the seat. "Of course I'm different."

He started to laugh. "Sarai, I told you before, and I meant it. You are uncommonly beautiful. Men stumble over themselves to make you smile. If anyone needs a buggyload of character to face that kind of special treatment, it's you." He shot her a smile. "And you have it, for the record. You're one of the best people I know."

"Oh…" She looked disconcerted then.

"Look, I'm not going to be trouble for much longer," he said, flicking the reins. "I've got to get back to work, and my grandfather needs to come with me."

"Unless he wants to stay," Sarai said.

"No, he needs to come." Arden gazed over at her soberly. "Look, he's not okay on his own. Can you keep this private?"

She nodded, and he pulled out the bills, passing them over. It was a strange relief to be able to share this emotional burden with her, at least. She flicked through the bills, her eyes widening.

"Oh, Arden… I didn't know!" she said.

"Yah."

"What will you do?" she asked.

"I'll pay it."

"Can you...?" She swallowed, and her cheeks reddened. "I don't mean to offend, but can you afford that? This is a lot of money owed..."

"I can just afford it," he said.

This kept happening. Whenever he got close to getting his savings built up enough to make things right with Job, he hit another obstacle. They turned onto the road, and he flicked the reins, speeding the horse up to a trot. It was nice to be driving in an area that was used to buggy traffic. It was less stressful here in Pennsylvania than in Ohio—at least in that respect.

"It doesn't seem fair that you have to pay it, though," she said.

"I'm the one here," Arden said. "I'm the one who has to do it. But you can see that my grandfather needs to come home with me, right?"

"I can see that he can't do this alone..." Her tone was quiet and even agreeable, but he noticed her wording. She wasn't accepting that Moe would have to leave, was she? Sarai would always be a force to be reckoned with.

"Moe loves Ellen, you know," Sarai said after a moment of listening to the horse's hooves.

"*Love* is a strong word," he said.

"And I don't use it lightly," she replied. "He loves her. I daresay that, at his age, if he's forced to part from her, he'll decline."

And that would be on his shoulders, too, would it?

"Sarai, what am I supposed to do?" he demanded. "I'm one man! And not a rich one."

"I know," she said.

"What solution is there?" he asked. "Your *daet* is a

good man, but it isn't fair that he be supporting everyone else around him, either. I won't be a burden on your father. Maybe we can help our grandparents write letters back and forth and help them visit each other. I don't know. But this is all I can do."

"We can pray," Sarai said. He looked over at her, and she gave him a small smile back. "It's really quite a powerful option."

"Yah," he agreed. "Then we'll pray for something to come along."

But for all his praying in the past, all he'd ever gotten was that daily bread. Gott's ways were not his ways, and Gott seemed to be intent on teaching him a lesson about getting just what he needed and not a scrap more. What made him think that He would answer with more now?

Sarai waited in the buggy as Arden went into the bank. When he came out and got back into the driver's seat, he looked sober. They set off for their first stop, the dry-goods store. Arden went in alone, the bill in his hand, and a few minutes later he came back out, silent. They did that for every single bill in the pile, Arden going into the store with money and the bill, then returning looking graver and graver.

By the last stop, the creamery, they went inside together.

"Good afternoon," Haddie Ebersole said with a smile. Her fourteen-year-old son, Timothy, poked his head out of the back of the shop.

"Mamm, the Troyer order is done," he said.

"Thanks, son." She cast him a smile, then turned her

attention back to Sarai and Arden. "Sarai, I have your grandmother's order here."

"Danke," Sarai said. "That's why I came."

Haddie turned her attention to Arden. "Arden Stoltzfus? Are you back in town? My goodness, the last time I saw you, you were thirty pounds lighter. You've grown up."

"Yah. Hi, Haddie," Arden said with a bashful smile. "I'm here to pay off my *dawdie's* bill."

Sarai stepped away to give him privacy. But she did notice that the thick wad of bills had dwindled down to just a few left, and when he counted out the last of them onto the counter, his hands were empty.

She'd never experienced that before—having no money at her disposal. Cash was never even necessary for her, and she realized in a rush that she was just a little bit spoiled that way. She'd never experienced the lack of anything, and here Arden was, giving his last dollars to pay bills that weren't even his.

When they left the shop and got back up into the buggy, she looked over at him.

"I'm sorry," she said.

"That's life," he said, and he picked up the reins.

"It's not fair, though," she said.

Arden just held the reins but didn't flick them. The horse shuffled his hooves, waiting.

"If a man doesn't have ready money, he can still have two things," he said. "A job to support himself, no matter how humbly, and his self-respect. I've got both."

He flicked the reins then, and the horse started forward with a jingle of tack.

And not for the first time, Sarai wished that Arden would let her father help his grandfather instead of taking the burden on himself like this. But she understood. Arden was a man now, no longer a boy in the community. It was time for him to take care of his own family.

"What will you do now?" Sarai asked.

"I'll have to have a serious talk with my grandfather," he said. "It's time to face facts."

She nodded, but a lump rose in her throat. He was going back home to Ohio, and Moe would go with him. She and Mammi would be alone in that house, and their happy days of visiting with Moe would be over... Sarai's time with Arden would be over.

She hadn't meant to get attached.

She'd been serious when she said that without Mammi, Moe might seriously decline, but it occurred to her now that Mammi Ellen might experience the same thing. What happened to an old person when the one they loved was taken away?

"Arden, if we can find a way for our grandparents to get married—if they want that—would you support it?" she asked.

"Hmm?" It seemed like his mind had been elsewhere.

"If Moe loves my grandmother and my grandmother loves him, would you set aside your pride and let my family support them together?" she asked.

"It's not about pride..."

"It is about pride," she countered. "If Moe marries my grandmother, then he's our family, too. And I think it would only be right to let us help them."

"Your *daet* might start getting tired of all these people he's got to support," Arden said.

"Then you don't know my *daet* very well."

"He's a good man," he replied. "But he's still a man,

and every man has his charitable limits. I don't want to press on his."

"But if they want to get married?" she asked hopefully.

"I don't think they do," he said. "After all these years, they're just friends, Sarai."

"They're from a different generation," she said. "They show it more quietly. They aren't so obvious."

He looked over at her, and that dark gaze of his smoldered with something deeper. Her breath caught, and he smiled faintly. "Like what I feel when I look at you. I'm not saying anything can come of it, but I am saying that I wouldn't be able to have tea with you for years on end and not do anything about it, either."

She stared at him. Had he meant that? She licked her lips and swallowed.

"Sorry if that upset you," he said.

"I'm not upset," she breathed.

"Good. Because it's true. My point is, when people feel something, it doesn't just sit there for years. So maybe don't get your hopes up for our grandparents."

"Oh…"

Was she being naive? Or was he being cynical? She wasn't sure, but her heart suddenly felt much heavier than it had before.

Maybe they all needed a win for love. Maybe Arden needed to see two happy old people kept together, just to show him that it could happen. And maybe, just a tiny bit, to prove her right.

When they got back, Sarai went back into the house and discovered Mammi Ellen alone in the kitchen doing some dishes. Arden's tool bag sat next to the staircase. Sarai would have to return it to him.

"Where's Moe?" Sarai asked.

"He was tired and went home," she said.

"Oh… I thought we were all going to have pie," she said.

"Where's Arden?" Mammi asked.

"He went home, too."

"See? Sometimes plans change." But there was something in Mammi's voice that betrayed sadness. What plans was she talking about? Was this only about pie? If Sarai knew Moe at all, it took a great deal to keep the man away from Mammi's baking.

"What's wrong, Mammi?" Sarai asked.

"I'll miss him, dear," she replied with a tremor in her voice.

"Did he say he was going?"

"He said he'll probably have to. He has quite a few bills, you see."

"I know."

"How would you know?" Mammi asked, shooting her a sharp look.

"They were Arden's errands today," she replied. "He was paying off his grandfather's bills. They had piled up. That's how I know. But Arden made me promise not to say anything about them. But since you knew about them already, I didn't see how it would hurt."

"That's very decent of him to help his grandfather like that," Mammi said. "I have your father's help, and yours of course, but Moe doesn't have the support I do. I know how blessed I am."

"He emptied his savings," Sarai said. "I think it took

a long time to save it up. I saw his face as he paid all those bills, and it…it hurt him to do it. Although, he didn't want anyone else to do it, either. I feel terrible for him, but Arden won't accept help with his grandfather."

"Oh, my… He has male pride," Mammi said.

"That's what I told him. It's awful."

Arden's pride stood in the way of simply sorting things out. She could understand him, but why must he be so stubborn about it?

"Oh, my dear, I don't mean it in a bad way. A man's holy pride is what makes him stand next to you with his shoulders back and his eyes blazing. His Gott-given pride is what makes him work his fingers to the bone to provide for his wife and *kinner*. It's what makes him choose the right instead of the wrong when it's easier to go wrong. There's a good kind of pride, and it gives a man backbone."

"Well, it's going to take both of them back to Ohio," she said.

"It might," Mammi agreed.

"And I think you and Moe love each other!" she said.

Mammi nodded. "We might."

This was it. Sarai had to do something. She picked up the pie on the counter.

"Mammi, I'm taking this pie over to Moe's place," she said. "We promised the men pie, and I intend to deliver on that."

"I'm doing dishes, dear," Mammi said. "And I think that Moe has made his peace with this. He'll miss me terribly, but he knows what he has to do."

What he had to do. What was being forced upon him. Was that a man's pride making him do what he thought he had to, even when it broke his heart? Mammi might see the noble side of it, but there was a foolish side, too. Pride certainly did go before a fall, and before heartbreak, too.

"I'll go alone," Sarai said.

"You want to see Arden," Mammi said with a sad smile.

"*Yah*, I do." That was part of it, at least.

"All right. Go ahead."

Besides, Sarai had to lay this out for Moe. It was time to shake these two old-timers and make them face their feelings. They loved each other—Sarai was certain of it. But Mammi would never speak first. So Sarai would have to do it for her.

As she marched out the door, Sarai realized she'd left Arden's tool bag behind. That was okay. This visit wasn't about Arden, anyway. It was about Moe and his feelings for Mammi.

Sarai arrived on the Stoltzfus step with a pie in a basket, which she held in front of her. She'd never been nervous to pop by Moe's house before, but suddenly, her heartbeat was skipping along like a stone across water. She was still sure that she was right about this, but Moe wasn't a man who welcomed intruders into his life, either.

She knocked, and the door opened after a minute to reveal the old man wearing slippers. He looked sad and tired, too.

"Sarai," he said. "Hello. Come inside. How are you?"

"I'm doing pretty well," she said, following Moe in. "How are you?"

"I'm quite tired this evening," he said.

Obviously, Moe wouldn't talk about this, but she might be able to get him to open up. She handed him the basket.

"I come bearing pie," she said.

"Danke."

She stepped into the kitchen, and she spotted Arden at the table, a boot in one hand and a jar of black polish open in front of him.

"Hi," he said, starting to stand.

"It's okay," she said. "I actually came to talk to your grandfather a little bit."

"Should I give you privacy?" he asked hesitantly.

"No, no," she said. "Stay where you are."

Arden sank back into his seat and picked up his rag again, rubbing the boot with the blackened cloth.

"What can I do for you, Sarai?" Moe asked kindly.

"Well, Moe, it's this..." Sarai took a quavering breath. "I think—" She swallowed. "I really think—"

But, staring at Moe, bringing out the words was a lot harder than she'd imagined it would be. Moe raised one eyebrow. She might have to come at this sideways, she realized, and she pulled out a kitchen chair opposite Arden and sat down in it.

"Moe, it's like this," she said. "I think you'd make a wonderful husband to...to someone. You're still very strong, and you're smart, and you're funny, and I've seen firsthand how very kind and attentive you are." She might be wise to pause and see how this was landing, but she didn't dare. If Moe stopped her now, she wouldn't be able to finish her speech. "Older men understand how to keep a home happy. They have wisdom and intelligence. Younger men really could learn from a man of experience like you. And I don't think you should be shuffled off to a bedroom with family. I'm just going to say that, and I'm sorry, Arden—" she looked over at Arden helplessly "—it's just how I see it. And I'm not going to pretend otherwise. Arden wants you to go home with him because they love you. I daresay everyone wants it very badly, but what do you want, Moe? You deserve a choice! And my family will be very happy to help support you and your... your wife." She smiled hesitantly. "If you were married, Moe, you'd have support. You wouldn't be alone, and I know what a truly remarkable husband you'd make. I know I'm young, but I'm able to see it."

Moe stared at her, his mouth open. He seemed to realize it, and he shut it. She glanced at Arden, and he looked equally amazed at her speech. Had these men never seen a woman speak her mind before?

"Moe, I just want you to think about it," Sarai said. "There is a woman who loves you. You know that—you aren't blind. And if you leave, she'll miss you so terribly, you have no idea. But she's afraid to say it."

"I think you've spoken quite eloquently, young lady," Moe said at last.

"Have I?" She smiled. "Good! I'm glad. Moe, you aren't used up yet. You have a lot of life and love left in you."

"Sarai," Moe said, folding his hands in front of him and fixing her with a tender look, "you are so young..."

"I know, but I'm not a fool, and I know what I see," she said.

"My dear girl, I know how it looks. I'm older, wiser,

more experienced… You think that I'd be an ideal husband because I'm mannerly. But, my dear girl, I'm *old*!"

"It's just a number, Moe."

"No, it's a lot more than a number. It's arthritis, wrinkles and about sixty years your senior. I have great-grandchildren your age. I'm flattered, Sarai. I truly am. Any man would be lucky indeed to marry you and set up a home. But I'm well past that age to be living the life a young woman like you would want to lead. I know this will be hard for you to hear…"

Wait. Something had gone wrong here, and it was Sarai's turn to stare at Moe in shock. Arden's shoulders were shaking with laughter, and he actually snorted into his hand! Did Moe think she was speaking for herself? She opened her mouth, but nothing came out, and Moe just kept on talking.

"You need a man your own age, Sarai. You need a man who will grow old with you, not an old man you'd be taking care of. I know that a man your age might scare you a little. They haven't quite learned all their manners yet, have they?" Moe cast Arden a wry look. "But I only became the man I am in my late wife's hands. You'll love your own husband the same way, and when he's my age, he'll be just like me. But that takes many years together."

"Moe—" she started.

"Now, Sarai, I can't let you go on like this." Moe reached out and took her hand in his own soft fingers. "Don't say another word… I know you'll find a man your own age. I'm sorry to turn you down like this. Your grandmother might be able to explain things better to you. But believe me when I tell you that I'm not the man for you." He released her hand. "I'm truly sorry."

Sarai stared at Moe in humiliated silence. She had done something very wrong here…

"Sarai, maybe you and I could go outside and talk?" Arden murmured at her side. She looked up at him in surprise. He must have come around the table without her noticing. He put a strong hand under her elbow and boosted her to her feet. His eyes twinkled with humor, and his lips twitched.

"*Yah*, okay," she said weakly.

Sarai followed Arden to the door, and when she looked back, aghast, at Moe, he put a hand over his heart and bowed his head.

That sweet, gentle, kind old man who she was trying to set up with her grandmother thought she'd just proposed marriage to him!

And he'd turned her down flat…politely, but flat.

Chapter Ten

Arden grabbed Sarai's hand and led her away from the house and straight across the yard toward the apple trees. Grass-scented air pulled him forward, and he refused to look back, lest he be forced to make eye contact with his grandfather. He'd never be able to do it and keep a straight face!

A bumblebee buzzed up from the grass and bounced against Arden's pants, and a host of sparrows flapped up from a nearby copse of trees like a sheet, billowed and then flew off in a low, black streak across the farmland. It was a beautiful day to stroll, but Arden didn't slow down. Sarai stumbled, but he tugged her past the apple trees with their low-hanging, rosy apples—not ripe yet, but they smelled tangy already—and into the knee-deep grass beyond them. Then Arden burst out laughing.

He couldn't help himself! He was chuckling about the ridiculousness of the whole scene. Sarai and Moe had both been so intent on saying what they meant to say,…and they just wouldn't stop. He couldn't help but laugh, because he knew no real feelings were at stake here, and both would be feeling very silly before the day was out.

Sarai just stared at him, stunned. Her cheeks were pale, and it would seem that what had happened hadn't quite landed for her yet. But she looked so endearing that he squeezed her hand and stopped short of pulling her closer.

"Sarai, you are very sweet," he said.

"I am?"

"And very earnest," he said with another peal of laughter.

"What happened in there?" she asked, and he heard the wariness in her voice.

Okay, maybe time to stop joking.

"I don't think you want to hear this," he admitted.

"Want to or not, I'd better hear it…"

"Okay, then." He caught her gaze and held it. "I think I'm right in saying you were trying to speak for your grandmother, not for yourself?"

"Of course! Wasn't that clear?" she asked, shaking her head. "I've told you from the start, I want my *mammi* and your *dawdie* to see what they mean to each other."

"No, it was not clear at all," he said. "It sounded very much like you were telling him that you wanted to marry him yourself!"

Sarai blinked at him and shook her head. He nodded back.

"It really sounded like I wanted to marry your grandfather?" she gasped. "Even to you?"

"*Yah*. Very much so."

"Oh, no!" Sarai pulled her hand out of his and rubbed

her hands over her face. "I realized he wasn't under-standing me at the end, but I hoped it wasn't my fault…"

"Well, he thinks he turned you down and broke your heart," Arden said. "He also thinks I'm out here talking you out of wanting to marry a very old man."

Color bloomed across her face, and she started to laugh then. "What have I done, Arden?"

"You've made an old man feel very young again, I can assure you of that," he said with a low laugh. "In fact, I wasn't going to tell you this, but every time you brought up marriage in front of my *dawdie*, it kind of sounded the same. Like you were telling him that you were thinking of him for your own husband."

"How could I?" she demanded. "He's a *dawdie*!"

"I know…but you didn't really make that clear. You kept telling him how much he had to offer, how wonder-ful he was, how polite and how much you liked having him around…and most recently, how your family would be happy to help support the two of you."

"Not the two of *us*, the two of *them*! I was trying to tell him that he should think of marrying my *mammi*, not me."

She groaned and then dropped her forehead against Arden's shoulder. He couldn't see her face, but she smelled nice, and this close to him, he was noticing how the sun played off her honey-colored hair. If he'd been Dawdie, he would have accepted her proposal in a heartbeat.

"It's not so bad!" he said, wrapping his arms around her. She fit nicely there—the perfect fit, really. "Just think of the story my grandfather can tell from this. He'll make you look like a dream and himself look like an old fool, and anyone who hears it will laugh until they cry."

He put his hands to her face and lifted her chin so that he could see her properly.

"I'm not sure that's better," she said, lifting her face. She still had spots of color in her cheeks. He wanted to make her feel better, break through the embarrassment she was feeling.

"Come on—it's a bit better," Arden coaxed. "I have to say, you're lucky I wasn't the one you were accidentally proposing to. I might have accepted."

He grinned down at her. That should do it—break the embarrassment. She was very close, and he could feel the heat in her cheeks against his fingers. If he'd gotten this close to Sarai years ago, he would have stolen a kiss. In fact, he was thinking about it now.

He should move back. He should drop his hands, at least…but she wasn't moving away from him, and he couldn't force himself to, either. Arden let his finger run along her jawline, and his gaze dropped down to her lips. She was beautiful—always had been. Everyone knew it. Strangers couldn't help but notice it. And here he was, with this beauty in front of him. But he could see something that no one else could upon first look: he knew her heart.

"You're teasing," she said.

"I'm being honest." But he grinned to soften it. It was better she not know just how sincere he was when he said he'd have jumped at her offer. "Go on, tell me I'd make a wonderful husband. I dare you."

"I will not!" She raised that laughing, glittering gaze to meet his, and his heart skipped a beat.

"Really? Are you sure? Because I'm very susceptible to that kind of flattery," he said jokingly.

She stood straight, still just inches from him.

"Arden, you are very, very good-looking, but—"

And that was really all Arden needed. He didn't want to hear the rest of it. He'd made her laugh, made her feel better, and in order to stop her from finishing that thought, he dipped his head down and caught her lips with his. He surprised himself when he did it. He hadn't meant to—in fact, if he'd thought it through for five seconds longer, he wouldn't have done it, but here he was. Sarai seemed surprised, too, and she sucked in a quick breath through her nose, but then her eyes fluttered shut, and he moved a couple of inches closer. Her lips were soft, and her breath was warm against his face. Now that she was in his arms, he didn't want it to end, so he slid his hand around her waist and wished that time would freeze. Sarai broke off the kiss, and for a couple of breaths they just stood there, their lips a whisper apart. She didn't move away, and neither did he. But when he leaned in to kiss her again, she put a hand against his chest, and he stopped.

"No," she whispered.

He straightened. "Sorry."

"Are you really?" She eyed him, a smile tickling her lips.

"Not terribly," he said, and he smiled back. "I'm sorry if I upset you. But you're wonderful, and I wasn't playing games—whatever you might think of me. That's the most honest kiss I've given any woman."

"We can't do this, Arden," she said, and her voice caught. Was she feeling more than she wanted him to see? He searched her face, looking for what, he didn't even know. He just wanted to know what she was feeling. Be sure of it.

"Maybe we could," he said hopefully.

"Arden…" She looked at him like he might be joking, and he knew he'd better back off now. He'd already gone way too far.

"Okay," he said. Was he supposed to argue with her? She was right. He was leaving Redemption, and she was looking for a husband worthy of her. The next time their paths crossed, she'd likely be a married woman. It didn't matter if he hated that fact. She was miles above him, and he knew it. But he couldn't just leave it at that and let her think he was joking or playing around, because he wasn't.

"My *dawdie* might carry the memory of when a beautiful young woman wanted to marry him," he said softly.

"Arden…" She shook her head.

"But I'll always remember this kiss. Always. It'll be the memory I treasure."

Tears suddenly misted her eyes. "Really?" Then she shook her head again and blinked quickly. "I'm being silly. I know you, Arden. You're used to saying all the right things, and it won't work with me."

"I don't know if that was right," he said. "But it's true. You're the most beautiful woman I've ever met, and I mean that after having gotten to know you."

"There you go again…" she said breathlessly.

Arden looked down at her, and his heart suddenly did something it had never done before: it closed around her. And as soon as it happened, he knew he was in trouble.

Because Sarai wasn't for him, and he wasn't for her, but she was still the most extraordinary woman he'd ever met. He cleared his throat and took a step back.

Sarai's fingers fluttered up to her hair, and she touched around her face, checking for any loose strands. She was putting up her defenses again, solidifying her armor.

"So…will you clear this up with Moe for me?" she asked, lifting her gaze to meet his.

She could have asked him to swim an ocean and he would have agreed. This was nothing.

"Of course," he said.

"Danke." She swallowed. "I'd better get back home. Mammi will wonder what's keeping me."

"And you'd rather not explain this?" he said.

"I'd rather not." She smiled then, and her gaze softened to tenderness. "See you later, Arden."

He longed to keep her there, but he knew she had to go, so he let his hand drop from her waist and watched as she headed back across the grass. His grandfather appeared in the window, and then the old man disappeared.

Yah, he'd have to explain to Dawdie. Moe would be relieved, of course, and then he'd feel foolish, and then Arden was going to have to bring up that conversation about the bills.

Because no matter how much Arden wanted to stay in this in-between world with Sarai and Ellen and the best pie in Pennsylvania, he couldn't.

Real life was waiting, pressing, demanding.

His honest talk with his grandfather about the financial realities couldn't wait any longer. But just for one more moment, he allowed himself the indulgence of watching Sarai in her pink dress as she walked across the grass toward her own home, her head down and her white *kapp* gleaming bright in the sunlight.

Sarai hardly saw anything as she walked across the field. Her mind was spinning, and her lips were still a little moist from where Arden had kissed her. But he hadn't just kissed her…she'd kissed him back! And he'd said he'd always remember that kiss, and the problem was so would she. Arden Stoltzfus was not the kind of man to take seriously—at least, he hadn't been in the past—and here she was, longing to turn around and go back to him…longing for another kiss.

What was wrong with her? She wasn't supposed to fall for Arden! His sweet words were supposed to be meaningless… And yet there was something much deeper there between them. Or was she just as foolish as every other girl who'd cried over him?

When Sarai went back into the house, she found her grandmother in the sitting room, her knitting on her lap. Her fingers were knobby from arthritis, but she still worked quite quickly, the needles clicking as she knitted.

"Hello, dear," Mammi said. "Did you bring back the basket?"

"No." She sighed and sank onto the couch next to her grandmother. "I forgot it. Sorry."

"That's okay. We know where it is. I'm sure Moe will bring it by."

"Mammi, I went over there to tell Moe that you love him," she said.

"You did what!" The needles dropped from Mammi's fingers.

"Before you get mad at me, it didn't work out that way," Sarai said. "Moe was under the impression that I was the one in love with him, and he thought I was proposing marriage."

Mammi started to laugh. "He didn't!"

"He did," she said.

"He didn't...accept your proposal, did he?" Mammi asked, her smile slipping.

"No, he didn't," Sarai said. "He gave me a very lengthy talk where he told me that he was far too old for me and I needed to focus on men my own age."

"He isn't wrong," Mammi said, and she started to laugh again, shaking her head. "You should focus on men your own age. I will talk to Moe when I'm ready, Sarai. I'm a grown woman. I know my own mind."

"Okay," Sarai said. "I'll leave it alone."

"Sarai, why does this matter to you so much?" Mammi asked. "Are you bored? I'd understand you wanting something more than this. I've been thinking for a while now that it's high time you got married and started your own family."

"My biggest reason is wanting to see you and Moe happy together," Sarai said. "I do think you care for each other, and I wanted to see that blossom. But secondly... I was hoping to go to Shipshewana to see Uncle Jonah and Aunt Lovie. They want to start a flock of specialty hens, and I could help with that—"

"And meet some eligible men at the same time," Mammi finished.

"Yah..." And it had seemed like a much rosier op-

tion before that kiss. She wanted to go find a respectable man in Shipshewana, not fall for the least appropriate match here in Redemption. But she'd fallen for Arden… badly.

"My dear girl, why didn't you tell me this?" Mammi asked, reaching over and taking her hand.

"Because you need me here," Sarai said. "And I won't go anywhere as long as you need me."

"That's just plain silly," her grandmother replied. "There are more members of this family than just you, and I won't have your life held back because of me."

"I knew you'd say that," Sarai said. "That's why I didn't tell you."

"So you think Moe will take care of me," Mammi said.

"I think you and Moe would take very good care of each other," Sarai replied. "I see how much happier you are when you're together. I see how you deflate a little bit when Moe leaves after he's come for dinner. How he gets a little hop in his step when he's coming across the field to our place. I think you make each other happy."

"We do," Mammi agreed. "But that isn't your problem, Sarai. I want you to go to Shipshewana and help your aunt and uncle with their flock and find yourself a wonderful man to marry. That's what I want."

Sarai was silent. Her heart suddenly felt very heavy at the thought. It would mean leaving whatever this was with Arden behind. She should. It was the smart thing to do… This thing with Arden had sprung up quickly, and she couldn't let her heart lead right now.

"Isn't that what you want?" Mammi asked.

"I thought it was," she said.

"Well, I still think it's a good idea," Mammi said. "You need to get out there and experience some new things. I know Jonah and Lovie would enjoy having you there, as would your cousin. And there are plenty of eligible young men who are probably praying to meet a girl just like you. Sarai, I want you to go. I think it's a good time for you to do it."

"What about you?" Sarai asked. This had never been her plan, to leave her grandmother alone.

"I'll be okay. Gott always provides something, and you don't have to take everything onto your shoulders." Mammi squeezed her hand.

"What if you have to move out of your house?"

"Then…I will face it."

"But I don't want you to face that!" Sarai said. "Maybe Gott will bring my husband here."

"I want you to go to Shipshewana." Mammi's voice firmed. "Tell me you will."

"Do you think it's good for me?" Sarai asked. "Honestly?"

"I think it's the right next step for you," Mammi said.

Her grandmother was right, of course, but Sarai couldn't promise. That had been her plan for a couple of months now, and every time she'd thought of it, she'd been excited about the possibilities. Arden had a life in Ohio, and he was needed there. He would certainly go back. Maybe it was better to go sooner, before her heart was any more entangled.

There was a knock on the door, and Mammi put her knitting aside and stood up.

"I'll get it," she said gently. "But remember, Sarai, when you feel like this—pent-up, frustrated—it doesn't mean there is anything wrong with your life right now. It doesn't mean you're making mistakes. It just means you're ready for the next step in your life. This is actually a very good sign. You're growing out of this little cocoon."

Mammi made her way through the sitting room and toward the kitchen. Sarai heard the door open, and then Moe's voice mingling with her grandmother's. This was not a rare occurrence. The older people would often drop by and borrow things or just chat. And perhaps he wanted to recount the story of her inadvertent proposal in a way that would save her embarrassment.

Sarai pushed herself to her feet and headed in the direction of the kitchen, but as the voices became clearer, she stopped in her path.

"My grandson needs me to go home with him," Moe was saying. "The truth is, Ellen, I don't have enough money left to keep this farm going. Arden used his own money to pay my bills. I'm embarrassed. Truly and deeply."

"Oh, Moe…" Mammi's voice was low. "I hate growing old."

"Me, too, Ellen."

"Will you go with him, then?"

"I might have to, but the thought of leaving you behind… What if I picked you up and put you in my hat and brought you with me?"

Mammi laughed softly. "I wish you could."

"Sarai came by—"

"She told me." There was a smile in Mammi's voice. "I misunderstood. Arden explained. Apparently, she was hoping to plant the seed of marriage to you in my head."

"*Yah*, she was."

"Ellen, I don't know quite how to say this. At my age, I should be sinking into my rocking chair."

"Oh, pssht!"

"Well, I don't want to leave you behind—ever! And I've grown to love you over the years, but I was afraid to say anything, lest it change our friendship."

"Well, it certainly would," Mammi said. "I've been waiting for you to say something, and you never have!"

"Wait…" Moe's voice muffled. "Wait. Are you telling me you have…a special fondness for me?"

"That's what I'm saying, Moe."

"What if we did the craziest thing?" Moe asked. "What if we did just what Sarai is suggesting?"

"And got married?" Mammi's voice shook.

"*Yah*."

"Are you asking me to marry you?"

"*Yah*, I think I am. Ellen Peachy, would you marry me? I don't know how we'd do things, exactly, but if we lived in one home instead of two, I think we might manage. What do you say?"

Then silence. Sarai held her breath, waiting for her grandmother's answer, but there was nothing. She crept forward and stopped at the doorway to the kitchen. She peeked inside, and there, standing next to the kitchen table, was Mammi Ellen and Moe. Mammi's hand was on her throat. Sarai pressed her lips together and tried not to make a sound.

"*Yah*, Moe… I will."

Moe clasped her hand in his and drew it up to his lips in a trembling kiss.

"You might as well come in, Sarai," Mammi said, not raising her voice or even turning. "I know you heard all of that."

Sarai couldn't say anything because there were tears in her eyes and her throat was tight. She crossed the kitchen, put an arm around each of them and pulled them into a hug.

"Thank you for the nudge, Sarai," Moe said when she released them.

"You're welcome, Moe," Sarai said. "I'm just so happy for both of you."

Mammi's lips quivered, and tears shone in her eyes. "A bride, at my age!"

"At our age, the sooner the better," Moe said. "We have details to discuss, my dear."

And that was Sarai's cue to leave the couple alone. They had plans to make together, and Sarai headed for the stairs to her bedroom, but as she passed Arden's tool bag, she looked inside. The light fell just right for her to see a little piece of paper. She bent down and pulled it out. It had been crumpled and the blue ballpoint pen writing was obviously Susie's because it laid out her name and address.

Sarai's heart hammered in her chest, and she took the slip of paper with her as she hurried up to her bedroom. What did this mean? She'd just kissed this man! Had he lied to her? Had he been up to his old games after all?

She sank into the chair next to the window and looked outside.

She closed her bedroom door, her pulse hammering

in her throat. Her mission was accomplished. Mammi and Moe would be together, and they'd be able to make each other happy for the rest of their days. Not only would Mammi and Moe want time alone, they'd need it. Even if Sarai stayed in Redemption, it would be time for her to move out of her grandmother's house.

She looked down at the paper again. He'd said it was all Susie. He'd said it wasn't him. Was there about to be another young girl sobbing her heart out over Arden Stoltzfus? Some might say Susie had it coming, but Sarai disagreed. Susie was young and foolish, true, but Arden should know better by now!

What was Sarai even doing? She'd always been smart and kept her head on straight. But whatever had been blossoming between her and Arden had felt real… It had felt like honest feelings between two people who truly cared for each other.

Downstairs, she heard her grandmother laugh, and it sounded an awful lot like a giggle. She couldn't help but smile.

Thank You for blessing Mammi and Moe, Sarai prayed in her heart. *And while You are blessing them, Gott, please also show me the truth about Arden. I fear I've been duped by him, too.*

Chapter Eleven

Arden had finished the chores, and he hadn't seen his grandfather for a few hours now. Normally, Dawdie came back to at least check on Arden. He liked things done a particular way, and he never seemed to trust anyone to do it just right. But he hadn't returned.

Arden's mind had been on his own finances when he'd had that frank discussion with his grandfather. He had no more savings left. That meant that he couldn't go to Job with a few thousand dollars in hand and begin the process of paying him back, and that rankled him. He needed this off his conscience, but Gott wasn't providing a way. Why not? Arden was truly sorry for his youthful folly, and he wanted to fix it—be a man about it. Why couldn't this be any easier?

What choice did he have? He'd bring Dawdie home with him and start saving again. Eventually, he'd be able to pay Job back, and this time, it would be his top priority. Nothing would deter him.

In the meantime, though, Arden needed to see Sarai

one more time alone. So Arden headed across the grass to the Peachy place.

He'd kissed her. He should probably apologize for that, but he wished she could see how honest that kiss had been on his part. He wasn't trying to take advantage. He wasn't playing games. His heart was in this... even though he couldn't do anything more about it.

So was he just as bad as she must assume—kissing her when he knew he had to leave?

But maybe she'd wait for him. That was the one fluttering hope inside of him, even though he knew that would be a choice she'd likely regret. He had a good deal of money to save up before he was square with her father, and he had no right to ask anything of her. And he hated that.

Arden arrived at the house and knocked on the screen door. The door was open, and he could hear voices from inside. His grandfather was laughing softly, and so was Ellen. They sounded incredibly happy... Why? How?

"Come in, come in!" Ellen called, and Arden opened the door. He stepped through the mudroom and emerged into the kitchen. Sarai and Ellen were both in work aprons, and Moe sat at the table, wreathed in smiles. Ellen's face was pink, and she looked younger, as if time had almost reversed, as she energetically worked with a rolling pin and some pie dough. But Sarai, standing next to her chopping apples into a bowl, frowned, her emotions looking more complicated. She met his gaze, and his heart almost skipped a beat at the sudden depth in those dark eyes.

"Hello," Arden said, and his own voice sounded a little strangled in his ears.

"Arden!" Dawdie half stood. "I meant to come back and talk to you, but I suppose it's just as well you came here. We have news." He settled back down into his chair.

"Oh?" Arden asked hesitantly.

"I've asked Ellen to marry me," he said with a broad smile.

"And I said *yes*," Ellen supplied from where she stood at the counter, rolling the dough.

"You're—" He licked his lips, his head spinning. "But, Dawdie, how?"

"We'll sort it out," the old man replied. "We'll live in one home together, so that will cut down on expenses. I'm sure your uncle will be happy to take over the farm early, if that's what it comes to. But Ellen and I will be able to figure things out, so long as we're together."

"Well—" Arden stepped quickly forward and shook his grandfather's hand. "Congratulations, Dawdie. Many blessings to you."

"This will actually work very well for my own family," Ellen said. "Sarai will be going to Shipshewana to spend some time out there, and that means that Moe and I will be alone. We'll take care of each other. And no one else needs to be inconvenienced."

Arden went toward Mammi Ellen, and she put down her rolling pin, wiped her hands on her apron and came around the counter to give him a hug.

"Congratulations to you both," he said.

"*Danke*, Arden," Mammi Ellen said with a smile. She patted his shoulder and headed back around to her piecrust.

"I'd like to say we could help financially, but—"

"Arden, dear boy," Dawdie said. "It'll be okay. I won't need it. You'd be surprised how thrifty two old-timers can be when they have each other."

"Plus, as always, I have my son's tab to rely on," Ellen said. "I never take advantage, but he'd be deeply offended if I didn't use it when I needed it. I raised him, loved him and kissed his scrapes better. He says now it's his turn to help make things better for me. And I truly appreciate his generosity."

"I'm very happy for you both," Arden said.

And he meant it. He was truly happy for them. He couldn't think of a nicer wife for his *dawdie*. Ellen was a gem, and he was happy they had each other. But it would mean that his family's inability to provide for Dawdie would be even more magnified. Job Peachy would be called upon to do his duty yet again, and that hardly seemed fair, especially when the groom for this marriage was a Stoltzfus.

All the same, his family's ability to financially support Dawdie in this next phase of his life wasn't the point today. He'd simply have to let his father know the news and go back to trying to save up the money to pay back Job.

Sarai was silent, and her gaze flickered up to meet his again, and he swallowed.

"Sarai, could I—" He nodded toward the door. "Could I talk to you?"

Sarai put down her paring knife. "*Yah*, of course."

"Take your time, *kinner*," Dawdie said, pushing himself to his feet. "I'm an old hand at slicing apples. I'll take over."

"Well, how nice," Ellen said with a beaming smile.

Sarai rinsed her hands, dried them, and then they headed outside together. Behind them, he could hear the low voices of their grandparents talking to each other.

"So you did it," Arden said as they walked away from the house together. "You got them together."

Sarai didn't answer, and he ducked his head to get a better look at her face.

"Are you mad at me, Sarai?" It was the kiss, wasn't it? He'd crossed the line, and she'd had time to think about it.

Sarai pulled a piece of paper out of her apron and handed it to him. He recognized the crinkled scrap.

"This isn't what it looks like," he said.

"Isn't it? You're going to be writing to her. Or at least she thinks you will be."

"That's not true. I told you before—she was flirting with me. I wasn't welcoming it. I was trying to send her back to the women, and I suppose I wasn't very successful. But I wasn't encouraging her."

"She gave you her address."

"And I crumpled it and dropped it into my bag," he said. "I meant to throw it out when I got back home."

She looked down at the scrap and seemed to be considering.

"I'm telling you the truth," he said. "I wouldn't lie to you, Sarai. For anything. I've told you the worst of our family situation, haven't I? I even told you about your father's buggy. Why would I start lying now? If I was a liar, I'd have started long before now!"

She stopped just past the chicken coop and turned to face him. A tendril of hair slipped free from her *kapp*. She didn't notice, and he liked it, so he didn't say anything. The chickens were scratching in the dirt in their enclosure, their throaty clucks calling to each other.

She nodded at last. "Okay."

He shook his head and closed his eyes. "Good. I'm glad. And you managed to get our grandparents together."

"Are you upset about that?"

"No. I told you I'd support it if he wanted to get married. And he obviously wants it."

"*Yah.* I'm glad they see it."

He smiled faintly. "Look, it's not easy for my family. I'm embarrassed we can't make things easier for them ourselves. But all the same, I'm glad they'll have your family's support." He looked over her shoulder, back toward the house. He couldn't see them in the window, but he could remember how they looked together. "They're happy."

"Deliriously." She looked over her shoulder at the house and then turned back to him. "No one expects you to impoverish yourself, Arden."

"We could have provided for him if he came back with me," Arden said. It seemed important that she know that.

She nodded.

"And we might figure something out yet. Maybe we'll find a way to build a *dawdie haus* on our property and bring them to Ohio in a couple of years."

"I suppose we could all share our time with them," she said, but her voice still sounded sad.

"And you'll tell me right away if they need to move in with someone, right?" he said. "We could bring them into our house easily. We'd make room."

"I know."

This wasn't what he wanted to talk about, though. Not really. They could plan for all sorts of scenarios: it wouldn't touch on this ache in his heart.

"I…will have to go home," he said at last. "Soon."

Sarai swallowed. "How soon?"

"Tomorrow."

"Oh…" Her voice was flat. "That's very soon. I was hoping for a few more days."

But a few more days would only make this harder. He'd fallen for her, and time would only solidify that.

"I thought my grandfather would have a difficult goodbye. It turns out it's me who will have a hard time walking away," he said.

"Will you?" She swallowed.

"Walk away?" he asked. "I have to. My job is waiting. My family needs me—"

"I meant…" Her face pinkened. "I meant have a hard time doing it."

He caught her hand and tugged her a step closer. "I hate it. I hate having to go and having to say goodbye. *Yah*, this is terrible. Is that what you want to hear?"

"*Yah*. Exactly." She smiled, but her eyes misted.

"Then you have it," he said. "I came here on a mission, and I thought if I just stayed focused on that, I wouldn't feel more for you. It didn't work very well."

"I'm sure you're used to this," she said.

"Used to what—loneliness?" he asked.

"Walking away. Cutting the strings. Turning your back," she said.

"That isn't what I'm doing," he said.

"You'll forget about me soon enough." She felt the

tendril of hair against her face, wound it around her finger and then tucked it up under her *kapp*. And then he saw in unflattering clarity exactly what she thought…

She thought she was another in a string of women he'd treated badly. He would never be able to get rid of his history, would he? Even when he'd fallen for a woman, she'd have trouble believing him because she'd seen him behave so badly in his youth.

"You think so?" Arden demanded. "How is that even possible? If you think I'm playing games with you, you couldn't be more wrong. *Yah*, I was a fool before. I toyed with girls' feelings, but Gott has a way of teaching a man a lesson. He doesn't leave us in our foolish mistakes. I was determined to do better in Ohio, but Gott wasn't done with me. He taught me a lesson with Mary. He showed me what it felt like to be used and dumped. It hurt, but I learned from it. And with you? This isn't pretend. This isn't just biding time. This is real…for me, at least. You're everything I've been praying for in a woman, Sarai. Everything. So maybe Gott is still showing me what pain feels like, because now I have to walk away, and it's the last thing I want to do."

Sarai swallowed, her breath caught in her throat. Arden stood so close, the heat from his chest emanating against her. His hands were rough, and he held her fingers firmly in his grip. She could see the sincerity in his brown eyes. This was no game…

The hens kept scratching in the dirt, and one settled down into a fluffy little puddle of feathers in a corner, clucking contentedly to herself. If only Sarai's life were that simple.

"Really?" Sarai whispered.

"Yah..." He pulled her closer still and rested his forehead against hers. "It's the honest truth. I love you."

Her breath seeped out of her, and she stared at him in shock. Arden's face colored, and he shrugged uncomfortably. Was that what this feeling was—the deep longing to be with him, the way he'd settled into a part of her heart that she'd never known existed before? The thought of going to Shipshewana didn't make her excited anymore because it meant leaving behind Arden and whatever this was that was growing between them. Whether she was here in Redemption or in Shipshewana with her extended family, she'd be thinking about one man... Yet he was the man she'd only very recently suspected of bad behavior with Susie. She couldn't just hand her heart over to him, but at the same time, he'd utterly ruined her adventure for her, and it made her want to cry.

Sarai had had a plan—she'd had Shipshewana, and now her grandmother would be happily cared for and Sarai wouldn't be missed at all. It would be perfect, except that she'd now fallen for Arden! If only she'd managed to keep him safely pigeonholed as "handsome but unworthy." Because now she was inclined to believe that he was worthy...

"Should I not have said that?" Arden asked. "But it's true. I fell in love with you. You're wonderful, and I'd love nothing more than to be the man who makes you happy."

"You love me?" she breathed.

He nodded. "It's okay if you don't feel the same way.

I know I'm not exactly the kind of man you were praying for, and I get it—"

"Arden!" She grabbed his hand again, and he squeezed her fingers hard. She couldn't have him think he was the only one feeling this, even if it couldn't work. But he was right—there was a word to describe all she felt. "I love you, too."

"You do?"

"Yah." It was simply the truth—whether it was wise or not. She loved him!

"Good…" His voice was low and gruff, and he pulled her into a kiss. She leaned into him, twining her arms behind his back. If she could have put everything she felt into that kiss, she would have, but she didn't know how to say it. Arden had slipped past her defenses, and she'd fallen in love with him.

When they pulled back, she blinked up at him, her heart pounding. He looked at her, and they didn't seem to have any more to say. They'd said it all—they loved each other, and he was leaving. What more was there?

"Then why don't you stay?" she asked, pulling back so she could look up at him.

"Sarai…"

"You could," she pressed. "Why not stay? I'm sure your family would understand."

And if he stayed, there'd be more time for her to see him behave well. She needed that—the reassurance.

"Sarai, my family needs my income," he said. "And I told you, I can't come here unless I can pay back your *daet*. If I can't come back and hold my head high, how can I court his daughter? I owe your *daet* a debt, and I promise you, I won't stop working until it's paid. I can even promise you I'll wait for you…but I can't ask you to wait for me."

"Why not?" she demanded.

"Could you really make that sacrifice for me?" he asked.

"Maybe…" But uncertainty was already worming up inside of her. She had an image in her mind of Lizzie crying into a handkerchief, saying she was so sure that Arden had felt something more for her…*something*.

"What holds you back?" he asked, meeting her gaze.

"Arden…" It seemed cruel to say it out loud when he'd already told her he loved her.

"Say it," he said. "I think it's important that we say it all. Something is holding you back, too."

He was right—something was. She was hesitant to trust her own heart on this.

"Because other women, better women than me, have cried their hearts out over you," she said. "And I'm afraid to be just another one of them."

He nodded slowly, pressing his lips together. "You aren't. And I didn't flirt with Susie."

"I believe you about Susie. But the others thought they were special, too." She cleared her throat.

He'd said many beautiful things today, and she believed him…didn't she? Was she truly different from every other woman? Could she be the one to captivate his heart for the rest of his life?

"I get it. I understand. But I need you to hear what I'm going to tell you. You have my whole heart. I've never felt this way before, and I don't expect to again. But it's more than that. I don't think I deserve you. You're miles above me, Sarai. Everyone knows it—

even I know it. You're kind, smart, beautiful, and you've never played the games I used to play. You're untarnished, and I fully understand you not being sure about trusting me."

"Because I can't?" she whispered.

Was that his gentle way of letting her know he was just as unreliable as she feared?

"No, Sarai. You could trust me with your life," he said earnestly. "But I'd have to prove it to you first."

"I wish we had more time," she said.

"Me, too..." He smiled sadly. "I wish I could just bring you home with me. But I'm going to pray that Gott will give me the ability to save up that money so I can pay your *daet* as quickly as possible. And when I pay it off, I'm going to come back and knock on your door."

"How long will that take?" she asked.

"I don't know," he said, his voice shaking. "Maybe years. Maybe decades. But I'll come say hello, even if I'm talking to a married woman with five *kinner*. I'll still come and tell you I paid him myself."

"What about Shipshewana?" she asked.

"You should go," he said. "Don't hold back your life because I failed to pull mine together in time. I'm going to pray for Gott to do something, but what could I tell your father if I asked you to hold off on all the good things because I couldn't pay him? That's not fair to anyone, least of all you. This is my problem, not yours."

"Not mine?" she demanded, a lump rising in her throat. "How can you say that?"

"I'm sorry." He stared at her miserably. "I knew I shouldn't let myself fall for you, because I've got nothing to offer. This is all my fault. I'm truly sorry. If it were just my heart in the wringer, I could endure it. But I dragged you into this—"

"No…" She shook her head. "As much as I would love to blame you, I'm a woman who makes her own choices, Arden. I'm here for the same reasons you are."

"And if I paid your *daet* back tomorrow…" He paused, searching her face. "If I were able to pay him back, would you be able to come to Ohio?"

"It's a hard life in Ohio," she said.

"Very hard. It's a lot of work out there."

"And you think I'm too spoiled to do it."

"I think you're too smart to take it on."

She smiled faintly. Arden was trying to give her a way out, and that was both infuriating and sweet. Because if he asked her to drop everything and go to Ohio with him, would she be able to do it? Could she trust her heart and her entire future to this man?

"It isn't the work, Arden," she said. "It's your history. I've comforted far too many girls who thought—just like I do now—that you cared."

"I do care," he said earnestly. "More than care. I love you."

Sarai might want many things, but when the horseshoes hit the road, she kept coming back to this question: Could she truly trust him? Would there be other women she wondered about, others who threw themselves at him like Susie had, or who Arden didn't push away as hard as he should? That was the part of her that was left stirred up and muddy inside of her. She loved him, but was he worthy of that love?

Maybe a few weeks in Shipshewana would give her time to think and untangle all of this confusion inside of her. Maybe with some time away from those piercing eyes and strong arms, she'd be able to see something she couldn't see right now.

"But until you repay my father," she said, "this is a pointless discussion."

He nodded. "*Yah*. Just know that if I had all of my hopes and dreams, I'd be with you."

Sarai heard the squeak of the screen door hinges, and she turned to see Mammi and Moe come outside.

"Sarai!" Mammi called. "Sarai?"

The timing was miserable, and she heaved a sigh. For all of her grandmother's happiness, Sarai's heart was broken.

"*Yah*, Mammi?" She didn't sound like her ordinary self. Her throat was tight, and right now she just wanted to cry.

"Moe and I are going to see your father to tell him our news," Mammi called. "Did you want to come?"

No, Sarai did not. She wanted to get away from here, though—to run and run and find some solitary place where she could cry and scream and let all these pent-up emotions out without having to explain herself to anyone.

"No, Mammi!" she said. "Go ahead. I'll be here."

Mammi Ellen and Moe set out for the stable, Moe holding Ellen's hand almost reverently. Sarai turned back to Arden, and for a moment they just stood there, listening to the clucks of the hens and the sound of Moe's voice as he spoke to the horse he would hitch up to Mammi's buggy.

"What do we do now?" she asked.

"I help them hitch up, and then I go back to my grandfather's house, and I get ready to go home," he said. "Before I do something stupid, like change my mind."

She nodded, and her throat seemed to close, allowing no more words. Arden bent down and pressed a kiss on her forehead.

"Goodbye," he whispered gruffly against her hair, and then he turned and strode off.

Sarai stood there, her heart hammering in her throat, and she wondered if she would ever feel this way again about any man. Shipshewana wasn't going to be the adventure she'd imagined. It would simply be a chance to get her balance back after heartbreak.

That wasn't what she'd wanted…

The hens clucked softly, and Sarai opened the door to the chicken yard and scooped up a red hen, shutting the door carefully to make sure none escaped. She smoothed a hand over the glossy feathers and looked down at the trusting chicken.

Gott, take this pain away, she prayed silently. *Let me stop loving him…please!*

But with every beat of her heart, she felt Arden getting farther away, and the only thing left to her was to sink down to her knees and let the tears flow.

She loved him—as foolish as that might be. Had she been weak? Had she been silly? Or had she seen something more in him after all?

Maybe Gott wasn't only teaching Arden a lesson. Maybe He was teaching her one, too, about the value of His children. Because there was so much more to Arden than the flirtatious ways of his youth, and she wished that instead of seeing the whole man and falling in love with him, she'd been permitted to stay naively ignorant.

Why did growth have to hurt so much?

She stroked the chicken, and her shoulders shook.

"Let me stop loving him," she said, sobbing. It was the deepest prayer in her heart.

Chapter Twelve

That evening, Arden paced the small ground floor of his grandfather's house. He tried to relax but had difficulty sitting down and thinking of anything besides Sarai. He knew that if he went back over there, there would still be nothing left to say, but he longed to see her all the same.

He had to stop this. He'd only been here for a week. She was right that he knew what breakups felt like. He'd had plenty of them. But Sarai was different, and he knew it.

Eventually, Dawdie came back, and Arden went out to help him unhitch. It was already late, and his grandfather had dropped Ellen off next door before coming home.

"You look really happy, Dawdie," Arden said.

"You look miserable." His grandfather squinted at him in the lantern light. "Are you all right? Is this about my engagement?"

"No, not at all."

"Because we'll figure it out, Arden. We will. I might be able to find a little bit of work and—"

"Dawdie, you're almost eighty-three! You aren't going to work," Arden said.

"All I'm saying is we'll figure it all out. And I know your father had plans to have me move to Ohio, but I'll write him a letter to send back with you. He won't hold this against you."

"Of course he won't," Arden said.

Arden led the horse into his stall, and when he came back out of the stable, his grandfather was waiting for him with the lantern.

"Then why do you look like your heart has been torn out?" Dawdie asked.

"How tired are you?" Arden asked wryly.

"I'll make us some tea," Dawdie replied. "It looks like you could use a listening ear, and I'm here for you."

They went inside together and made a pot of mint tea. Sitting at the table across from each other, Arden laid it out: how he'd fallen for Sarai, how he loved her, but how she was struggling to truly trust him, and he owed her father the amount of money it would take to buy a new buggy.

"What would help her trust you?" Dawdie asked.

"Dawdie, it's more than that. I owe her father!"

"*Yah*, but that's just money," Dawdie replied. "This is more important, I think. What does she need to trust you?"

"She needs—" Arden shook his head. "I think that if I had her father's respect and I paid him back properly to get it, she'd be more comfortable. I can't just whisk her off and marry her. She comes with a family—the same family you're marrying into!"

"Yah, yah..." His grandfather looked down thoughtfully at the table. "Have you talked to Job yet?"

"About this?" Arden laughed uncomfortably. "Until I can walk up and hand him the money and look him in the eye, I don't dare."

"You can look him in the eye without a cent in your hand," his grandfather replied. "Respect does not come with money."

"True," Arden said. "But it also comes without debt."

"It helps..." His grandfather rubbed a hand over his white beard. "But this is between men, and it isn't really about Sarai yet, is it? I think you need to go to Job, confess what you did in your teenage years and ask his forgiveness."

"I'll be easier to forgive if I'm also making restitution," Arden said.

"There is right, and there is wrong," Dawdie said. "When you have done wrong, you have to ask for forgiveness. Perhaps that is the key to unlocking the rest of your life."

"I know I was wrong. I was a foolish *kind* in a lot of ways, Dawdie. I hurt a lot of people, and I don't need to be shown my error. I can see it plainly! I just... I have to be able to make it right. Don't you understand that?"

"It's pride," his grandfather replied.

"No, it's a need to fix it!"

"Which is pride." The old man raised his bushy eyebrows. "True contrition is simply going to your Christian brother and asking that he forgive you. Repayment comes later."

Arden rubbed his hands over his face. "Maybe it is pride, Dawdie. I've lost anything I might be able to feel proud of. In Ohio we struggle constantly. There's nothing easy over there. I don't want to come as the failing son of a failing farmer."

"You won't," Dawdie Moe replied. "You'll be going as the hardworking son of a hardworking farmer who is doing his best to start a new community to benefit new generations of Amish *kinner*. You are not failing because it isn't easy. You're simply working hard. You only fail if you quit."

Arden looked at his grandfather tiredly. "And you think I should go as I am and ask Job to forgive me?"

"Yah."

He sighed. "I hate when you're right, Dawdie. I will certainly be going with no pride left at all."

"We tend to be at our best when we leave the pride behind," Dawdie said. "Now, go to bed. Everything looks better in the morning light."

Arden stood up. "I'm sorry to drag you down on your celebration day."

"Arden, this is what grandfathers are for," Dawdie said. "Now, I mean it. Go to bed. We'll wash our mugs in the morning."

So Arden did as his grandfather said, and he went to bed. He didn't think he'd sleep at all, but he fell asleep in an exhausted heap the moment his head hit the pillow. Heartbreak needed rest, too.

The next morning, Arden helped his grandfather with the chores, and then he hitched up the horse to the old buggy and headed out in the direction of the Peachy farm.

Job's farm was large—the biggest Amish one in the

district. It had five good-sized greenhouses, acres of crops and a decent-sized herd, too. It took a lot of work to run, which was why most Amish farms were smaller, but it also made a good income, and Job Peachy was known for being a solid Amish deacon, as well as a well-off farmer.

Arden was dreading this visit, but he knew his grand-father was right. Gott had stalled things in Arden's life, and perhaps He was trying to get Arden's attention about this unfinished matter. Mistakes were tempting to walk away from, but they kept dragging along be-hind a man if he didn't deal with them.

Gott, give me the strength to face him, Arden prayed.

Arden pulled into the long drive, past a large pro-duce stall complete with a gravel parking area that was already busy with several customers being served. He nodded to the teenagers who were working there, and he carried on down the drive toward the big house. The grass had been recently cut, and petunias bloomed in tubs along the drive. Mature trees provided welcome shade, and in the distance he saw cattle grazing.

Would Job even be nearby? He could be anywhere on his farm this morning, and he wondered if he'd be able to get away with a piece of pie with Job's wife and put this difficult conversation off for another day, but then he spotted him coming out of the stable with a bucket in one hand and rubber boots on his feet. He looked up and shaded his eyes as Arden reined in his horse.

"Good morning!" Job called.

Arden jumped down from his buggy and sucked in a nervous breath. There was no chance of avoiding it now.

"Good morning," Arden called back.

Job put the bucket down, peeled off his gloves and headed in his direction.

"We saw your grandfather last night," Job said when he got closer. "We're happy for them. Your grandfather is a good man, and I'm glad my mother found love again."

"*Yah*, they're very happy," Arden said. "I wish we could do more to support them as they start out—"

"No need to worry," Job replied. "I already support my mother. It won't change much, actually."

"All the same." He dug his boot into the gravel. If he didn't say it now, he never would, and he grimaced. "Job, I have something I have to tell you."

"Oh?" Job crossed his arms over his chest and sobered. "What is it?"

"Five years ago, your buggy was stolen for a joyride and was totaled," Arden said.

"*Yah*, I know. That was a good buggy, too. I was sad to see it go that way."

"I wanted to come see you with the money to pay you back for it when I confessed to this, but life didn't turn out that way. All the same, I think I need to confess. I was the one who stole your buggy and took it for a ride. I was the one who ruined it. It's been on my conscience for years, and I told myself I'd save up the money to replace it. I haven't managed that yet. Every time I get close, some expense comes up, and it gets put off. But I want you to know that I'm going to pay you back. It will happen, but first, I have to humbly ask your forgiveness for what I did."

Job was silent, and Arden swallowed hard.

"I know," Job said at last.

"What?"

"I saw you return the horse and run off," Job said. "I knew it was you."

"You knew?" Arden shook his head. "You should have told my *daet*, had me punished or something."

"No, you were old enough to know what you did was wrong. Punishing you wasn't going to convict you of anything," Job replied. "But I knew it was you, and I saw how miserable and scared you were when you brought the horse back."

"Then…it isn't any surprise to you," Arden said. "If I'd known you knew, I would have come to you sooner. But I am sorry. I feel terrible for what I did, and I will pay you back. I just…hope you can forgive me."

"I forgave you when you did it," Job replied. "Anger and resentment are too heavy for a man to carry around. It was a good buggy. I was sad to have it ruined, but it was replaceable."

"Then you understand why I can't accept help for my father's farm," Arden said. "I owe you, Job, and I take that very seriously."

"You do not owe me," Job replied.

"I do! I won't rest until I've paid you back. I have to be able to look you in the eye as a man."

"You do that already," Job replied. "You work hard. I've heard good things about you from one of the families out there. They say you're mature, dedicated and a truly decent man. Son, you grew up."

"I did," Arden said.

"You owe me nothing," Job said. "Let it go."

Arden wasn't sure what to say to that. This had been his goal for so long now that he couldn't exactly drop it.

"As a man, then, you'll understand why I need to pay you," Arden said.

"Do you have the money now?"

He shook his head. "I paid my grandfather's bills. And even before that, I didn't have enough saved."

"So you intend to scrape for another few years to pay me back?" Job asked. "Arden...you're right. You broke something that belonged to me, and by all standards, you should repay it. But I'm not facing you as a man to a man. I'm facing you as a Christian to a Christian, and I'm not holding you to what you deserve. I'm offering you grace. The same grace Gott offers me."

Arden felt tears sting his eyes, and he dropped his gaze to hide it. He kicked the gravel with one boot and swallowed hard. The burden was lifting off his shoulders, and he could almost feel his own back straightening again.

"If you put it that way..."

"And," Job said and put a hand on Arden's shoulder and gave it a squeeze, "I believe in what your parents are doing out there. I believe in what you're doing in Ohio. We need more Amish communities to expand into. This is an investment in our children's children. Gott didn't call me to Ohio, but I want to help you all get settled. I want to provide that down payment for the thresher, and a little extra."

"My *daet* will be very grateful," Arden said, his voice thick.

"I'm going to tell you something that I hope you'll remember in your own dealings with others," Job said quietly. "We have to allow people the space and the grace to grow. You needed to grow when you were a young man here in Redemption. Gott was not finished with you yet, but from what I've heard and what I see in front of me, Ohio has been good for you. That place grew you up and taught you some lessons. I'm proud of who you've become, Arden. You're a good man, you hear me? A good man."

"Danke." Arden sucked in a shaky breath. "I appreciate that more than you know."

"Now, if you wanted to stop in for a cup of coffee, my wife has been baking," Job said.

And how could Arden say no to the man who'd just forgiven him so much? But also…this was Sarai's father, and he was getting a rare opportunity to sit down with the man and get to know him on a different level. An idea had started to grow inside of him… Now that he was free of his debt, things might be a little different between him and Sarai.

He smiled gratefully. "I'd be happy to."

Maybe, just maybe, Job would one day be willing to welcome Arden into his family. But one step at a time…

An Englisher woman accepted the last carton of eggs from her order and placed it into a box in the back seat of her car.

"Thank you so much," she said. "I'll see you again next week."

"Yah. See you." Sarai smiled, but her chest still felt tight.

She hadn't slept well the night before, and she hadn't even told Mammi what had happened. She didn't want to ruin her grandmother's happiness right after her engagement. She looked like a girl in love—blushing and smiling and humming to herself while she worked.

The Englisher drove away, and Sarai walked back over to the porch where Verna waited, sitting on the step.

"Sarai, you look so sad," Verna said.

"I'll be all right." But she wasn't sure that was true, and she couldn't just lie to her friend, so she added, "Eventually."

"You fell for Arden, didn't you?"

A tear slipped down Sarai's cheek, and she dashed it away. "I did. But it was foolish of me. I'm no better than any of the others, am I?"

"Was he just playing games?" Verna asked with a frown.

"I wish he were," Sarai said. "I know **how** to be angry at him. But this was earnest and real **and** honest."

"Then what's wrong?" Verna asked.

"First of all, he can't come back because he needs to pay someone back for something, and…it's not my story to tell, and I promised him I wouldn't tell anyone. But he needs to pay someone back and he doesn't feel like he can come here until he does."

"Oh…" Verna frowned.

"And even if he'd paid them back, his family still needs him in Ohio, and if it weren't for his family needing him, maybe he'd stay here. And me going to Ohio is quite scary…" Sarai winced. "I suppose for me, it all boils down to the fact that I don't know if I can really trust his love."

"Because of his history," Verna said with a nod.

"Yah." Sarai sank down onto the step next to her friend, and Verna reached over and took her hand.

"I hope I wasn't part of you worrying about him going back to old ways," Verna said. "I know I reacted really quickly when I saw him talking to my niece, but she talked to me later, and she felt terrible. She'd been throwing herself at him, and he kept kindly telling her she needed to come back to us women. He wasn't taking the bait, Sarai. He was being decent."

"That's what he said, too," she said.

"So it's confirmed," Verna said.

"Maybe."

Verna was silent for a moment. "I shouldn't say anything, but I went to Bishop Glick this morning, and I told him about my worries about my niece. Arden came up, and in confidence, the bishop told me that they'd been hearing very good things about Arden in Ohio. He works very hard. He's reliable. He's honest and fair. Sarai, he's not the same as he was."

Sarai looked over at her friend, her mind spinning. "He really has changed?"

"It happens," Verna said. "Gott doesn't leave us the way He finds us. He improves upon us, and it seems that He has been working on Arden. He's more compassionate now, and he's careful in his affections and actions. You even said he needed to make something right with someone here in Redemption. That's not the boy I remember!"

"Me, neither," Sarai agreed quietly. But he'd never be able to pay her father back, and it all seemed utterly hopeless.

"Does he feel the same thing you do?" Verna asked.

Sarai nodded. "We love each other."

Verna put a hand over her heart. "Really?"

Sarai nodded again, not trusting herself to speak.

"You know how special that is, right?" Verna asked. "I'm older than you, and I've been praying for years for a good husband. Falling in love doesn't come along every day. It hasn't come along for me yet!"

Verna was silent for a moment, and then she turned toward Sarai. "Can I tell you something that embarrasses me?"

"Yah..." Sarai met her friend's gaze.

"I used to dislike Englishers." Color rose in her friend's cheeks, and Verna dropped her gaze. "I was very bigoted. I thought they were wicked and heathen and just willfully blind to Gott's ways. I didn't like them. I wouldn't talk to them at the market. I'd pretend I didn't understand them or that I hadn't heard them. I would glare at them and tell them to stop it when they tried to take pictures of me. I told myself it was because of our beliefs, but deep down it was just that I didn't like them, and it was an excuse to say something sharp."

"I remember you not being comfortable around them," Sarai said.

"It went deeper." Verna looked chagrined. "I'm only telling you this because I changed. Gott changed me, really. The bishop and that politician woman asked me if I'd teach the knitting class. I only started doing it because I needed the money, and they were willing to pay. I was scared at first. And I thought I wouldn't like them simply because they were Englishers. But that class changed me. I was forced to talk to those Englisher young people, and they told me their own stories. As I got to know them—the very kind of Englishers that scared me most—I realized that they were just *kinner*. And…I won't ever see Englishers the same way again. I'm not prejudiced anymore. They really are just like us. My point is people can change, Sarai. I did, and I won't ever go back to being the same way I was again. We grow and we learn over time. We become better people. By the time we're your grandmother's age, may we be as sweet and saintly as she is!"

Sarai looked at her friend thoughtfully. "I never knew you felt that strongly about Englishers."

"And I hope you won't tell anyone," Verna said. "I didn't talk about it openly, but it was in my heart. I'm embarrassed about my past attitudes. But if I can change, then so can Arden. And if he has, and if he's ready to be a devoted husband, then it would be a shame for some other girl to benefit from it."

The very thought of Arden marrying someone else was like gravel in her stomach, and Sarai wondered what her grandmother would think after all her earnest talk about going to see her aunt and uncle.

"I agree, but I was supposed to go to Shipshewana. I was supposed to look for a good match out there." Sarai swallowed. "I don't want to go anymore, but I'll have a lot of explaining to do, and I hate having my heartbreak laid out for all to see."

"But you wanted the adventure in Shipshewana…" Verna leaned her elbows onto her knees.

"You think I should still go?" Sarai asked miserably. "Because I don't want to anymore. It won't be the same. Anywhere without Arden was going to be painful. I think I need to get over him first."

"I don't mean you should go to Shipshewana, necessarily. If you want adventure," Verna said, "I hear Ohio is just brimming with it. There is nothing quite so adventurous as starting a new Amish community."

Sarai froze, her thoughts swirling. Ohio…with the hardships, the small community struggling to get a foothold, the Englisher neighbors who just wouldn't understand yet and the financial stresses that would certainly be waiting. Would she be willing to face a life without her father's credit in the stores, without all of the comforts she took for granted, in order to be in Arden's arms at the end of a day?

It wouldn't be an easy life. There would be no safety net of a wide and established community. If she sold eggs, the egg money would be for necessities and not her personal spending. It would be a whole new life. It certainly would be the next step forward, wouldn't it?

"I would need to learn how to shoot more than a pellet gun," Sarai murmured.

Verna nudged her arm and smiled. "I think you'd do just fine. If you could trust Arden, that is."

Sarai stood up, her heart starting to swell with hope. "I need to talk to him…"

Nothing might change. He had plenty of his own reasons to hold back, and she couldn't alter those. But something had changed for her, and she couldn't let him go back to Ohio without hearing it.

"I'm sorry to do this to you, but I have to go find Arden," Sarai said.

"Go!" Verna said, laughing. "I have a knitting class to prepare for anyway."

And Sarai started across the field toward the Stoltzfus farm. She'd say her piece before he left, and then the rest was in Gott's hands.

Chapter Thirteen

Arden stood in the stable, his heart pattering in his chest. He closed the stall door, and the horse tucked into a new manger of hay.

He didn't know how he'd tell Sarai what he was hoping… He had to figure out how. That was his problem. She'd already told him that she had plans to leave Redemption and that she didn't fully trust him. That was huge!

But he'd talked to her father today and chatted with her mother, and her younger brother had asked him about Ohio, and…and when he'd driven away from the Peachy farm, he'd just known that he had to try once more with Sarai.

Except, how could he ask her to go to Ohio and live so much more simply, giving up all the comforts of her family in Pennsylvania? Would her parents even approve? Surely, they'd hoped for more for her. Just because Job had been kind didn't mean he'd be willing to see his daughter married to him.

Which left Arden here in the stable, pacing back and

forth, trying to string together the feelings inside him into words. And it wasn't working.

"He's in the stable, I believe!" Arden heard his grandfather say.

Was someone here? He went to the stable door and pushed it open. Sarai stood there, her hands limp at her sides and her eyes filled with emotion.

"Sarai, are you okay?" he asked.

"I had to talk to you," she said.

"I had to talk to you, too," he said. "I was just trying to figure out how."

Dawdie stood by his rosebush where he'd been clipping some blooms, and he looked over at them with a smile.

"I'm just on my way over to see my fiancée," he said with a wink. "Don't mind me."

Arden chuckled, and Moe ambled off in the direction of the Peachy house. They'd be alone for a little while, at least.

"Sarai, I want you to wait for me," Arden blurted out.

"You do?"

"*Yah.* I need you to wait for me… I know it's a lot to ask, but I'll prove you can trust me. I love you, Sarai. I'm not the same fool you used to know. I'm a better man now, and maybe you could even ask your father about that. He said he's heard good things."

"So did Verna," Sarai said.

"Good, good! I'm glad. I'll make sure there's nothing but good to say about me, but I want to write to you and visit you and court you properly. The thing is, your *daet* forgave my debt, and he pointed out a thing or two about what it means to be a Christian man. I'm going to accept that kindness on his part, and I'm going to get my start in saving for a wedding."

"Oh, Arden…" Her chin trembled.

"And…and…" He cast about inside of him. "And maybe you'll start saving the egg money, too, if you could see a future with me."

"*Yah*, I can!" she said. "Arden, you did change. And I do love you, and I was quite afraid of taking a chance on you, but my grandmother pointed out a while ago that this pent-up, frustrated feeling is just being ready for the next step. I'm ready for that with you. You've become a good man, and I know it."

"Are you saying you'd come to Ohio?" he asked. "Would you come help us get the new community established?"

"I'm not as tough as the women out there," Sarai said.

"Maybe not," he said. "But I'll do my best to keep you comfortable. I promise that."

"I'm not that bad," Sarai said with a low laugh. "I cook, and I can shoot. I raise a quality flock of chickens, and I can sell eggs. That's a start, at least. I can garden and I can produce, and I'm not a great seamstress, but I'll put some effort into improving. I haven't lived quite so frugally as I'll have to yet, but I think I can do it."

"You'd be willing to?" Arden asked, tugging her into his arms. She felt so right in his embrace, her dress catching on the front of his pant legs. She looked up at him, her eyes sparkling.

"It would be an adventure, all right."

"But you're saying you'd come," he pressed. "Sarai, I need a clear answer here. I love you. I really, truly love you."

"I love you, too, Arden."

He was tempted to kiss her just then, but he needed that answer, so he held his breath, waiting.

"*Yah*, I'd come," she said at last. "But only after a proper wedding."

He couldn't help the grin that split his face. "Of course! That's what I want. I want to marry you, Sarai, and get down to the business of building a life together."

"Then you have to ask me," she said, a little smile teasing at her lips.

"Sarai Peachy, would you marry me?" he asked, and for a moment his heart refused to beat.

"*Yah*, Arden. I will."

Arden lowered his lips over hers and tugged her closer into his arms. This was all he needed: Sarai in his arms and a wedding on the horizon. He could work day and night for a life with her, and he'd do whatever it took to set up a home to provide for them.

When they pulled back, he looked down into her face and felt such a surge of thankfulness that it nearly shook him.

This was what Gott's grace looked like—the love of a woman he didn't deserve and the undying determination to live a life to make both her and Gott proud of his efforts.

Gott was very, very good. And he couldn't wait to start the rest of his life.

Epilogue

Sarai and Arden got married on a Tuesday in October.
Sarai and her parents had visited the Stoltzfus home
in Ohio that September, and they'd dropped off Sarai's
hope chest in the little addition to the family home where
she and Arden would be starting their married life. As
a special wedding gift to her, Arden had also built her
a beautiful large chicken coop to get her started with a
new flock of specialty hens.

Today, though, was the day that all of her and Arden's
planning would come together, and their life as a married
couple would begin. Leaves blazed in oranges and yel-
lows and crunched underfoot. The church benches were
all filled up with guests sitting shoulder to shoulder, and
there was a swarm of people in the standing-room space.
This was mostly from Sarai's friends, family and con-
nections, but Arden's family was here, too.

Sarai had two *newehockers* standing with her today—
Verna and Naomi, who had come all the way from another community in Ohio to be at Sarai's wedding for
her. Naomi's husband, Mose, was seated with the men,

and every little while he'd turn in his seat and glance toward Naomi with a look of such love that Sarai hoped she and Arden would be the same. He was protective right now because Naomi was seven months pregnant with their first child. She couldn't take three steps without Mose trying to help.

Sarai stood at the back of the tent next to a gas-run heater. Her blue wedding dress wasn't quite warm enough until the tent warmed up, and the blast from the heater was welcome. The day was chilly but bright with golden sunlight, and Sarai sucked in a breath, trying to find some calm.

"Where is he?" Sarai whispered.

Verna and Naomi looked around. Arden hadn't arrived at the tent yet, and Sarai's stomach knotted. All of her extended family was here, as well as his. Their friends and friends of friends who were excited about enjoying the first wedding of the season were all in attendance, lining the benches and whispering in anticipation. Young people would be hoping to meet their own match today.

"There," Verna whispered, and she pointed.

Arden had slipped in at the front, and he stood to the side with his own *newehockers*—his brother and his cousin. Arden's gaze swept the crowd, and when he saw her, a smile spread over his face in a look of relief.

He was here. The knot in her stomach loosened. That was all that mattered—that he was here. Everything else today could unfold any way it pleased. All she needed was for Arden to promise to be hers, and they could handle the rest.

"Let's get you up to the front," Naomi whispered. "See, Arden's heading for the chairs."

It would be a long service. There would be hours of preaching, singing, recitations...

Sarai let them usher her up to the front of the tent, where the bishop waited with an indulgent smile on his face. Her parents were already seated in the front rows with Arden's parents.

But it was when Arden turned and their eyes met that she felt like her knees might buckle. She sank into the chair that had been set for her, and Arden sat down in the wooden chair meant for him, a proper eighteen inches apart.

"Ready?" Arden whispered, and he shot her one of his heart-stopping grins.

She nodded. Vows would be said, sermons preached and songs sung. She'd remember very little of it. But this moment—looking at Arden as they got ready for this leap—was a memory that would always remain.

"I'm ready," she whispered back.

And she meant it with every fiber of her being. She was ready for anything life threw at them—challenges, happiness, long winters, hot summers and hopefully a houseful of babies to raise together.

She was ready for blessings—the obvious kind and the kind that came at a couple by surprise. She was ready for hard work, for struggles, for resting in her husband's arms and for growing their future together.

Because if there was one thing Sarai was absolutely certain of, it was that Arden was the man for her. Gott had reassured her of that over and over again as she prepared for this wedding. With Arden at her side and Gott leading, she could face anything.

Today, however, this beautiful life began with a vow. Would she promise to love and support Arden, honor and cherish him, as long as they both should live?

And the answer to that was as deep as her heartbeat.

Yes. She would be his. He would be hers. She couldn't wait!

* * * * *

*If you enjoyed this book by Patricia Johns,
pick up these previous titles in her
Amish Country Matches miniseries:*

The Amish Matchmaking Dilemma
Their Amish Secret

Available now from Love Inspired!

Dear Reader,

I hope you enjoyed this story. When I sit down at my computer and plan another book, it's always with you, my reader, in mind. So if you enjoy my books, I'd love to hear from you. It always gives me a boost to hear from people who have connected with my stories. Posting a review is a huge help, too, and I'm eternally grateful for every review my readers provide. I couldn't do any of this without you!

If you'd like a chance to win a package from me, join my newsletter! There is a link to it on my website at patriciajohns.com. You can also find me online on Facebook, Instagram and Twitter. I'm always around, sharing pictures, talking about books and just enjoying the company of fabulous readers.

I hope our paths cross!

Patricia

LICNM0723

Get 3 FREE REWARDS!

We'll send you 2 FREE Books plus a FREE Mystery Gift.

Both the **Love Inspired**® and **Love Inspired**® **Suspense** series feature compelling novels filled with inspirational romance, faith, forgiveness and hope.

YES! Please send me 2 FREE novels from the Love Inspired or Love Inspired Suspense series and my FREE gift (gift is worth about $10 retail). After receiving them, if I don't wish to receive any more books, I can return the shipping statement marked "cancel." If I don't cancel, I will receive 6 brand-new Love Inspired Larger-Print books or Love Inspired Suspense Larger-Print books every month and be billed just $6.49 each in the U.S. or $6.74 each in Canada. That is a savings of at least 16% off the cover price. It's quite a bargain! Shipping and handling is just 50¢ per book in the U.S. and $1.25 per book in Canada.* I understand that accepting the 2 free books and gift places me under no obligation to buy anything. I can always return a shipment and cancel at any time by calling the number below. The free books and gift are mine to keep no matter what I decide.

Choose one: ☐ **Love Inspired Larger-Print**
(122/322 BPA GRPA)

☐ **Love Inspired Suspense Larger-Print**
(107/307 BPA GRPA)

☐ **Or Try Both!**
(122/322 & 107/307 BPA GRRP)

Name (please print)

Address   Apt. #

City   State/Province   Zip/Postal Code

Email: Please check this box ☐ if you would like to receive newsletters and promotional emails from Harlequin Enterprises ULC and its affiliates. You can unsubscribe anytime.

Mail to the Harlequin Reader Service:
IN U.S.A.: P.O. Box 1341, Buffalo, NY 14240-8531
IN CANADA: P.O. Box 603, Fort Erie, Ontario L2A 5X3

Want to try 2 free books from another series? Call 1-800-873-8635 or visit www.ReaderService.com.

*Terms and prices subject to change without notice. Prices do not include sales taxes, which will be charged (if applicable) based on your state or country of residence. Canadian residents will be charged applicable taxes. Offer not valid in Quebec. This offer is limited to one order per household. Books received may not be as shown. Not valid for current subscribers to the Love Inspired or Love Inspired Suspense series. All orders subject to approval. Credit or debit balances in a customer's account(s) may be offset by any other outstanding balance owed by or to the customer. Please allow 4 to 6 weeks for delivery. Offer available while quantities last.

Your Privacy—Your information is being collected by Harlequin Enterprises ULC, operating as Harlequin Reader Service. For a complete summary of the information we collect, how we use this information and to whom it is disclosed, please visit our privacy notice located at corporate.harlequin.com/privacy-notice. From time to time we may also exchange your personal information with reputable third parties. If you wish to opt out of this sharing of your personal information, please visit readerservice.com/consumerschoice or call 1-800-873-8635. **Notice to California Residents**—Under California law, you have specific rights to control and access your data. For more information on these rights and how to exercise them, visit corporate.harlequin.com/california-privacy.

LIRLIS23

HARLEQUIN
PLUS

Try the best multimedia subscription service for romance readers like you!

Read, Watch and Play.

Experience the easiest way to get the romance content you crave.

Start your **FREE TRIAL** at
<u>www.harlequinplus.com/freetrial</u>.